# AFTER THE END OF THE WORLD

ERIC JOHNS

WALKER BOOKS
AND SUBSIDIARIES
LONDON • BOSTON • SYDNEY

Books by the same author

*My Life as a Movie Hero*

*Trip of a Lifetime*

For younger readers

*Capture by Aliens!*

First published 1999 by Walker Books Ltd
87 Vauxhall Walk, London SE11 5HJ

This edition published 2000

2 4 6 8 10 9 7 5 3 1



This book has been typeset in Sabon.

Printed in Great Britain by Cox & Wyman Ltd, Reading, Berkshire

British Library Cataloguing in Publication Data
A catalogue record for this book is available from the British Library.

ISBN 0-7445-7770-5

# CONTENTS

# *FIRST ENCOUNTER*

There's sweat running in our eyes and we can only gasp out what we want to say in short bursts. Ralf's got us in this state, of course. We're arguing in near-hysterical whispers.

"People!"

"What're they doing?"

"Let's go and ask them."

"Ralf! Wait."

"What for?"

"They might have the disease."

"That was fifty years ago, Cindy. They're alive. The disease has gone. Finished. Finito."

"I agree with Cindy. Observe first."

"You've been asleep for half a century, Chris. You've survived, man. Act for once."

Even then Chris mutters, "Christopher" to correct him, and adds: "Five minutes more won't hurt."

"You'll be dead before you finish observing."

"Please, Ralf."

"Hold Doug's hand, Fiona."

"You always were a stupid bastard," I tell him, which is what makes being with him exciting.

"Smile for the birdie."

"Where d'you get that?" Now he's annoyed me again.

"The store tunnel, of course. Where d'you think?"

"Who said you could?"

"Piss off, Cindy. You're not in charge – there's no one to tell us what to do."

"The stores belong to all of us," I protest feebly. He's as irritating as ever.

"You want it, come and get it."

Ralf waves the camera at the rest of us hidden in the trees and dances out into the field.

"Come back," Chris – aka Christopher – hisses. "You put us all at risk."

Ralf presses the hard copy button and tears the photo out of the camera. "Anyone want a snap of four moles frightened of daylight?"

"Ralf, they've seen you." Fiona's voice, birdlike, rises and vanishes.

"I'll tell them I'm from the local rag, come to do a piece about twenty-first century peasants." He lopes a little way into the field and raises his hand. "Greetings from the Age of Technology," he calls, and walks towards the ragged figures. They become motionless.

"I could bloody kill him sometimes," Doug

observes calmly.

I see Fiona's hand trembling. She clutches at his sleeve. "Don't say anything, please. Not while he's—"

"What're they doing?" Chris asks, squinting into the sunlight.

"Nothing." I move leaves aside. "Not even blinking."

Ralf shambles, loose-limbed, across the stubble towards the frozen tableau. I cross my fingers and swear at him under my breath. Lanky, sloppy, more fun than all of them put together, still over-confident of his ability to talk himself out of any mess his big mouth gets him into in the first place – even after fifty years. (Why not five? The question hangs over everything. We'd been told five.)

"Can you hear what he's saying?" Chris keeps repeating.

We strain, but only catch phrases through the hazy afternoon air. Ralf's city sharpness is out of place. He stands in front of the still figures. His voice swoops and mocks in an exaggerated greeting.

"I'm frightened," Fiona whispers. "Why don't they move?"

I can feel Ralf summing up the group of seven in front of him. Hayseeds.

"Friends, yeomen, countrymen," he declares, loud enough for us to hear. "I bring greetings from another time." There's no flicker of recognition. "I'm one of the good guys." Hand on heart. "Here,

I'll prove it." He raises the camera. They seem to stiffen. I know what he's saying to himself. Beads for the natives.

The camera whirrs. He turns the mini-screen towards them. He must have asked them if they wanted a hard copy because the next thing he does is tear off a photo.

The men stare at him.

We can hear enough to feel his impatience.

"What's wrong with you guys? It's a photo. A pic. That's all."

One of the group says something. A single word. "Say again?" Ralf demands, then shrugs uncomprehendingly and says something else.

The man in front suddenly shifts his weight from the pitchfork he's leaning on.

They're tired of listening to him, I think. But then the man casually raises the pitchfork and thrusts it into Ralf's stomach.

For a millisecond, as adrenalin surges, Ralf is silent as though he feels no pain through the shock. Then he screams, and as he sucks in his breath to scream again I see at the edge of my vision a blade skimming the stubble towards his legs. Rooks seem to rise out of his mouth like black hands.

I am staring, paralyzed. My mouth is open as if I'm helping Ralf scream.

Fiona's making little moaning sounds. Doug clamps his hand over her teeth and lips. She's shaking like an animal.

I find myself whispering, "No, no, no. Not Ralf.

Not Ralf, please."

"Run," Chris is telling us. "Run." He pushes me round, away from the sight of scythes directed down, point-first, at a patch of field. His face is ugly with horror.

We flee in a panic-fuelled, stumbling run back to the Base. All the way we feel eyes aiming at our backs. But there's no sign of pursuit, no sign that anyone knows of our existence.

# *THE AWAKENING*

Ralf's dead.

That's where this record of what they've done to me starts.

The bastards have killed him. I'm not talking about the peasants. You'll see who I mean when I've told you the lot – whoever you are. This is my digital message in a bottle. Not that I'm ever going to get rescued. I'm marooned in this medieval hell-hole for eternity. What I want is to put on record how I was used. Therapy, I guess; like lying on a couch spilling my dreams. The pigs who did this to me are all dead. But I'd still like to dig them up and garrotte them. That would be real therapy.

When we get back to the Base I don't even feel like eating. I suppose it's shock. I mean real shock. Like silver blankets round shoulders on the old disaster news channels. Only there isn't anyone to wrap me up. I have to get by on my own. Fortunately I'm pretty resilient, not like wilting orchid Fiona.

Doug is looking after her, of course. No, I do not fancy him. Big hunky types are not my fix. One of the sleepers is just what I fancy. I've been along to look at him a few times, naked in his capsule. Why shouldn't I? There's not much fun around here.

Types I like are Ralfs. They make things happen. Life's exciting with them around.

Anyway, that first day I'm in a state of shock so bad I turn in without having a shower or bothering about my hair, which is full of twigs, or my nails, which are absolutely vile from scrabbling over fallen tree-trunks.

I've ended up in the cesspit of history. What's someone like me supposed to do here? Get out, is all I can think of, and that's not an option.

I force myself to have a hot drink, and on the way back to my cubicle I pass Fiona's. The door's not closed so I grab a quick look, and there's Doug sitting on the edge of the bunk holding her hand while she stares wide-eyed at the ceiling, seeing God-knows-what.

But what's interesting is Doug. I can tell at a glance that he's not thinking about her. There's a hard, distant expression on his face, and it's not Ralf he's thinking about either. Whatever scenario he's running through his head, he's got the star part, and I'd give my last drop of hair conditioner to know what that is.

I walk past their open door and neither is aware of me. I'm just about to go into my cubicle when I hear Chris mumbling in his cubicle further down the corridor. I seem to be invisible, so I decide to look in on him as well.

Chris is kneeling by his bunk groaning. Wow! I think, what kind of sexual perversion is our uptight little moralist into? There's sweat running down his face. Then I hear what he's muttering and I'm *really* shocked. "Give me the strength to forgive," he's pleading, and I realize that Christopher-bloody-Robin is saying his prayers.

What have I done to deserve being marooned with this bunch of weirdos? I ask myself as I retreat to my cubicle and lock the door. When I am finally bunked down, I pull my sleepsac over my head and say goodnight and good riddance to this loony-bin for twenty-first century refugees and peasant psychopaths.

Then I get hot and start to suffocate, and I have all these pictures like freeze-frames in a movie flashing across my mind. Ralf, open-mouthed, falling, the camera arcing backwards. It's a silent movie, because I never hear any soundtrack of his one scream. I guess that's the shock.

I'm delirious with fatigue but I can't sleep. I decide to review the day's events, instead of sheep, and analyse what I know. I'm going to be in control from now on. Not wildly like Ralf. Coldly. I don't plan to end up kebabbed on a pitchfork, that's for sure.

I stick my head out of the sleepsac and take a few cooling breaths. Order and analyse, I tell myself. That reminds me of Hairy McKay saying,

"Yee've gort a guid brain, lass, if only yee'd use eet."

Always had a hand in his pocket playing with himself while he leant over and looked down the front of my shirt. And I always hunched my shoulders to make it extra loose. What he meant was, believe what we tell you and we'll give you prizes and certificates and make you a poxy prefect and turn you out a perfect little robot. Yes sir, no sir, three bags full of crap, sir. Well, I wasn't playing their games. So here I am now – no one to blame but myself, you say. But you don't know all yet. Anyway, I'm alive and they're dead. Or in McKay's case, deed.

I hear Mum pushing the Hibernation Programme to Dad. They both work for the University, but Mum is in the Vice Chancellor's department and has access to confidential information. Potential sleepers are not supposed to know what's going on until the selection has been made. Thinking back, I reckon Mum wanted me to overhear. She intended me to decide. Yeah, she knew what I'd do.

Dad's Mr Indecisive in person. I always get him to do what I want. He's given to outbursts of sentimentality. Like about my name. When I was small I was called Lucy. By the time I'm ten I feel sick every time I hear it, so I refuse to answer to anything except Cindy.

"We called you Lucinda," Dad drools, "because you were such a beautiful baby. We loved you very much and wanted a beautiful name for you."

"Well, you know what Lucy sounds like to me?" I say. "Loo seat, and I'm not going to be called that. No one's going to shit on me." From then on I'm Cindy, and Dad begins to latch on to the idea that I'm not going to turn out to be a fairy-tale princess.

At twelve I try to shorten it to Cin, but for once I don't get my own way. Mum goes hard. Probably as well, I think later. Don't wear a badge, except as a disguise.

Anyway, before being accepted for hibernation, I have intelligence tests and physicals and instruments shoved in so many orifices that anyone not in the medical profession would be done for child abuse. But I get to jump. The question is, why me? With my school record, I should have smelt a fifty-year-old decomposing rat.

I was suspended for swearing at teachers when I was seven, and again for hammering nails into Miss Shapiro's car tyres when I was nine. After that I'm old enough not to get caught. The school psychologist makes excuses for me. I'm bored because I'm bright. It doesn't take a genius to suss that out. I've read all the A level texts before I'm fourteen. But what I am is pissed off by stinking, sadistic, perverted, lobotomized teachers having power over me. So, since they wanted the best of the breed for hibernation – why little ole me?

There's nothing to hibernation after the jabs and the anti-bac meals (i.e. the embalming fluid you have to drink). You just go to sleep and, before you can count to ten, it's five years later. (Or, rather, fifty.)

When I wake up I think I'm still waiting to fall asleep. I count backwards to zero. Ten, nine, eight ... you know, that sad game doctors play. Beat the injection.

I dream myself saying, I did it.

Ten, nine, eight ... I do it again.

Why aren't I asleep? I wonder, and open my eyes. But she's not there. No doc. I'm alone with the moulded, transparent lid of my capsule pressing down on me.

I feel on the verge of uncharacteristic panic. But silently, because my lips are gummed. I'm trapped in a crystal coffin like Snow White. A fairy-tale princess at last, Dad.

I'm not fully conscious or thinking clearly.

Then the pins and needles start and it feels as though I've been lying on my arms and legs for years.

Five years! Realizing suddenly.

I'm being revived.

My first sound is a groan. It echoes in the capsule like an old car horn, one with a rubber bulb. I imagine I'm in an open-topped car. Goggles. People behaving too young for their age. Images flicker. Not my world. A life lived in videoland.

"It feels more like fifty years," I croak, and laugh with relief. An appropriately hollow laugh. Many a true word in jest.

When I push at the counter-balanced capsule lid I am nervous, like stretching a scar. Will my arms work? Wasn't there talk of the risk of muscle atrophying, of joints calcifying, of gangrene? The programmed movement of the capsule was supposed to prevent all that.

Exhilaration. All of me feels the same. Five years' suspended animation. I've done nothing, like on a birthday, but I feel as though I ought to be congratulated.

There are arrows along the capsule chamber which lead me to a door marked "Living Quarters". I pass through a shower. The water tastes of chemicals and the air from the drying vents smells musty. I come to a pile of loose robes folded on a shelf. My feet don't feel the floor. It's made of a composite material which is temperature neutral. Everything is state of the art. From this moment things begin to seem odd.

Labels to start with. Food, supplies, equipment. What everything is, how to use it.

I have a drink, several. I need to feel liquid running down my throat. Before I get any further, Chris comes hobbling in.

"Why's there no one here to meet us?" he asks, sounding peeved.

"You think the disease wiped everyone out?"

"I did think that for a moment. But look at this place. There was nothing like it here when we went into hibernation."

"Well. They got it ready afterwards." I shrug.

"It's better than the old hut which hid the entrance to the Base."

"Obviously," he says condescendingly. "But why go to so much trouble? This isn't just for resuscitation. You know where this equipment comes from?"

I don't, but I'm sure he's going to tell me. (He gets on my tits. Too intense with his call-me-Christopher fussiness. Not my type any more than Doug.)

"It's from the University Space Research Programme. They've built a space station in the quarry. It's a place to live – for years." His voice rises.

"Have something to eat. Then we'll work it out." My voice sounds relaxed. Other people's panic always makes me feel superior. Just like with dear old Dad.

Fiona and Doug join us. But it isn't until Ralf staggers into the living quarters that we stop talking and act.

Even when groggy, Ralf's more alive than the rest of them. He comes in with his arms stretched out like the creature from the crypt.

"Gee, Mom. Those sleeping pills were the real thing. Is breakfast ready?"

He drapes himself over me, casually squeezes a breast, and everything becomes a mad challenge.

"Go play with yourself," I tell him.

"Let's see what other toys the nice people have left us."

We nose into things. The Base is hidden in an old quarry, but while we've slept, the crater and the galleries off it have been transformed. There's a store tunnel, too long to explore; an assembly hall; seminar rooms; sleeping quarters; libraries of CDs, videos and even books; a games room; a multi-gym; recycling and hydroponic units; a control room; and everywhere warnings and instructions for operation.

The place is huge. It could be a space station cart-wheeling above the world and the tunnels could be spokes joining concentric fuselages containing everything necessary to support life. Why?

We walk round the observation gallery for the hibernation capsules. Through viewing panels we can see the other sleepers. We recognize some of them, but at the same time they are featureless, subtracted from.

"There's Tina," Doug exclaims. "I didn't know she was taking the sleep."

"Marty looks his usual lively self." Ralf pulls a face at an immobile figure.

"They're all older," Fiona says in a whisper.

She's right. When we hibernated these people were two years behind us at school. Now they've caught up.

"What does it mean?" Fiona does her appealing-to-Doug act.

"Those running the programme waited to see if we'd suffer any ill-effects before letting the next wave hibernate," he says bluntly.

Fiona shudders. "We were guinea pigs."

"What are we now?" I ask. "Why aren't the others waking up?"

"We're still guinea pigs," Ralf squeaks. "Tickle my tummy for me, Cindy."

"There must be a record of resuscitation times somewhere," Chris says disapprovingly.

We're just getting used to the sight of people like us lying dead to time in coffin-like capsules when we discover the desiccated corpse.

Fiona screams.

I get a twinge of contempt. It *would* have to be her who sees it first. She's known to her intimates as Fiddles, would you believe. How can anyone with even a micron of self-respect allow herself to be called that?

"It's horrible!" She's shivering.

"Don't look," Doug snaps, pulling her against him, while staring compulsively over her shoulder at the mummified figure.

"*Mama mia!*" Ralf exclaims.

"Shut your stupid mouth," Chris shouts, shocked out of his usual control.

It's Ralf's way of dealing with the situation. I'm tolerant in his case. Gallows humour. I think it's quite witty.

Did he manage a last wisecrack in the field?

"The life-support system must have failed," I say calmly. If you can keep your head when all around are losing theirs – then you're the one in control.

We reach the end of the gallery and find a panel showing capsule numbers with resuscitation dates next to each.

"Some of the waking times are out," I say, without really taking in what that means. It's methodical Chris who notices that all the capsule dates show fifty years after the date of hibernation.

"None of them shows five years," he says.

I watch the same thought form in all our minds.

"What numbers are our capsules?" I ask.

Ralf says, "One to five. The first in the gallery." Even he's subdued.

"They're all wrong," Fiona says faintly. "They're all wrong, aren't they?"

No one answers.

"What's going on?" Doug asks. "This isn't how we were told it would be. It should be five years and all of us together."

Big hunk. He likes things to be predictable, then he can plough on untroubled.

Ralf shrugs. "Look on the bright side. We get first choice of everything. I'll have the bed by the window."

"There aren't any windows," Fiona says helpfully, smiling so that the world won't hurt her. Tough luck, kid.

But even our sleeping cubicles have been selected for us and our personal possessions installed in a locker which can only be opened with our thumb print.

Suddenly Fiona gives a cry. "They're all dead!

Everyone we knew is dead. All our families..." Her voice quavers.

"If that date's accurate, my brother will be nearly seventy while I'm still fifteen." I'm more interested by the idea than frightened. "If he's still alive."

Mind you, none of it seemed real then, except to Fiona, who starts to look bright and distant. She's your actual blonde fairy princess. Tall, slender, beautiful and brittle Fiddles. I get a dreadful foreboding of boredom: she is going to be into nervous breakdowns. (How did she manage to pass the tests? Even at that early stage I began to think that something about the selection procedure stank.)

To us it's only been seventy-two hours since we saw our families. You can't see a few numbers on a display and accept that you've jumped from the first half of the twenty-first century to near the end.

"Are we still in the quarry?" someone asks.

Apart from the curve of the observation gallery, which might reflect the wall of the quarry crater, and the store passages, which resemble tunnels, everything is unrecognizable.

Doug nods. "We could have been moved while we slept."

"One way to find out." Ralf, of course. "Who's coming walkies?" and he heads off down a passage with an exit sign.

"Wait a minute." Chris's usual response. "We don't know what's out there."

"I'll let you know."

"Ralf's right. We've got to find out where we are as a first step." Doug supports him, cautious but not scared. Is there a calculating streak in him?

"Yes, but—" Chris, impatient at being harried.

"Come on, Mister Yes-but," Ralf calls back.

"We all go," I decide. Safety in numbers. Well that's what I thought then.

Ralf goes on ahead of us, but the security arrangements force him to stop. Beside the exit there's an intercom panel and instructions which provoke more questions.

"Keyword Operated Door" the notice tells us. "On first exit from the Base touch the red pad and speak the keyword you will use for re-entry. The keyword will be effective for any entrance."

Ralf puts on an act of making a mystic sign and intones, "Open sesame."

The door rolls aside. Beyond stretches an unlighted tunnel, once a quarry gallery. The end appears to be blocked by a shadowy rock wall.

"Wait," I order. "Ralf will go first to test the door from the other side."

Everyone seems happy to do as I say. A born leader, that's me. Or a bossy cow.

"One small step for yours truly," Ralf says, hand on heart. "One giant leap..."

The door closes ponderously behind him. The impression of weight suggests that the plastic sheath covering all surfaces is only a coating and that it conceals a grade A security system for the Base. Which leaves us all standing there wondering.

Waiting for Ralf seems to take longer than the sleep. When the door re-opens, Ralf staggers out of the gloom, one hand clutching his throat and the other clawing at it as though he's being throttled from behind.

"A fine, sunny day, folks," he announces. "It's pitch black when the door closes, but there's a fissure along the wall to guide you, and just before the outer door it ends in one of those round fossils."

"Ammonite," Chris mutters, like someone who is weary from correcting the world.

"Say the magic word and the rock opens." Ralf grins, but there's an echo of nervousness behind it. "If you'd just walk this way, ladies and gentlemen," he grunts like Dracula's servant, and limps off into the dark.

"Give a keyword," I tell the others.

"Steam," Doug says.

"Shalom," Fiona whispers to the intercom.

"Resurrection," Chris declares.

I choose, "Freedom." Big joke.

Ahead of us we hear Ralf say, "Open sesame," and the passage fills with sunlight.

It's a perfect morning, summer to judge by the foliage on the trees below. We feel our senses awakening properly for the first time. The assault of colours, sounds and smells drowns us. We really have survived the sleep.

We're on a rock ledge above a primeval forest which wasn't there when we came to hibernate.

The sky is a Union Jack blue. There should be a Spitfire doing a victory roll. There always is in videoland.

The outline of the ridge on either side of us confirms that the Base is still in the quarry. But there'd been fields and a lorry-wide track into the crater when we arrived. Plus a hut that looked like something quarrymen used, disguising the plastic and stainless steel implant which was our cocoon.

"It *is* fifty years," Fiona whispers for all of us.

"We'd better find some proper clothes," Chris says. "I'm not going exploring in a dressing-gown."

We laugh. The only time he's ever said anything amusing, and I'm pretty sure he meant it seriously even then. Disapproves of jokes for some reason, does our Christopher. He's a nonentity to look at. Fair to brown hair, pale green eyes, sharp features, white skin, thin mouth and wet lips that would make you puke to kiss. This world won't make any difference to him; he wouldn't enjoy himself wherever he was.

Later we career madly along a grass-covered ridge, crashing a path through brittle stems and scrambling over dry-stone walls cemented by weeds. Poor soil, I reflect from my geography lessons. No depth up here to support trees.

Then we sight smoke. It hangs like a drowning hand above the treetops three miles distant.

We plunge downhill, all the time following Ralf, who leaps and dances, a mad Pied Piper, luring us on with visions of a new land, of people sane and healthy, waiting to become sisters, brothers, fathers, mothers, lovers.

We thrash our way through trees and streams for hours, blinded by sweat, made hysterical by a need to find explanations; and eventually Ralf leads us to the inhabitants of this brave new world.

The first sight is a sobering douche. We've stumbled on to a movie set.

Ralf says let the cameras roll and plays his last scene. Fifty years waiting for that.

Mission accomplished. He's saved us by being himself.

Epitaph for Ralf.

I fall asleep at some point without fitting anything into a meaningful pattern.

# *BRAVE NEW WORLD*

Day 2 and I wake up saying, "Act. We must act."

We need information. That means getting out there and exploring.

What I intend to do is push the others into doing what I want. The one thing I'm sure about is that I'm not about to let anyone write me out of the script like Ralf.

I check outside before the others are up. A dull day weatherwise, and no excitement on the peasant front, I'm relieved to say.

After breakfast, when everything's been cleared up on my say-so – discipline's what they need – I tell them, "Right, we're not just going to sit here. Those scythe-wielding psychos aren't going to keep us penned up."

Fiona smiles. "I think we should just wait until someone comes. My father..."

God knows what the silly cow's on about. (Nervous breakdown's my diagnosis.) Doug squeezes her hand. I've already decided to let him handle her, in the nicest possible way.

"Cindy's right," Chris says. "We've got a job to do."

I didn't know I'd said that. But it's OK by me.

"The only question is, what is it?" Doug says, and I think I detect a mocking tone. There's something of the sly peasant about him, waiting to see initiative fail.

"Any ideas?" I ask Chris.

"You remember that when we looked at the other sleepers yesterday," Chris says frowning, "between us we knew all of them, didn't we?"

Doug and I nod. Fiona joins in. I hadn't said at the time, but I'd known every one of the sleepers. Not well, but at least by sight. I don't know why I'd kept shtum. Instinct. Always give yourself an edge. I've seen enough movies where they talk outa de side of de mouth to know that's good advice if ya wanna survoive in dis lousy woild. I just felt there was something odd about the whole set-up. (Looking back, I was right.)

"What I was thinking," Chris goes on, generously sharing his thoughts with us, "was that we are some sort of advance party. Our job is to explore and collect information."

"Then we provide reassuring faces to welcome the others when they wake up," I say.

"I think it's more than just welcoming them," Chris says. "I've looked at the dates on the capsules again. The next batch of five are due to wake in four months' time. Then the remaining thirty-nine four months after that, within a few days of each other."

"You think," I continue for him, "that whoever set this up fixed things so that if there was danger out there no more than five of us would be lost at a time?"

"Yes; and if after two attempts that method failed, then a mass awakening was ready as an alternative."

"Can you see our parents doing this?" Doug asks.

"If the situation was bad enough." Yeah, I could do something like this. No problem. "Perhaps they reckoned this would give some of us the best chance of survival."

"The disease must have got worse than anyone expected at the time we took the sleep."

"Is it just the disease?" Chris asks.

"What d'you mean?"

"Well, those people we stumbled on, they didn't behave like anyone we've ever met, did they?" Chris looks at me, wanting reassurance. "How many people have you met who kill on sight?"

(Intellectually speaking, there was Hairy McKay and the rest of the teachers' union.)

"You mean something's happened to change people so they don't behave the same way any more?" I ask.

"Something of the sort." Chris shrugs. "There's one more thing. The dates on the capsules are as easy to set as the timer on a video. We can change them if we want to."

"Why should we do that?" Doug asks mildly.

"Amongst the sleepers I know, there's a computer freak, a mechanical genius and a fitness fanatic. What we're supposed to do, I think, is explore and decide what special abilities are needed to increase our chances of survival, and then we revive the appropriate people. Those of us in the first groups, I'd guess, have a selection of skills useful for an advance party. Whatever they are."

I glance at Fiona and say amen to that. I've already decided that my special skill is going to be surviving by getting the others to do what I want.

"Unless anyone's got a better idea, I suggest we operate on the basis of Chris's theory and start by getting ready for a day's exploration. Agreed?"

Of course they agree. They've talked themselves into it. Anyway, who's going to disagree? Only Doug, and he'd rather see someone else fail than put his own ideas on the line. (Well, that's what I thought at the time.)

I fetch a camcorder from the store tunnel and record a message for the next five sleepers, saying what happened the day before and what we were proposing to do today. Just in case – there's security in superstition.

I am just finishing when Doug returns from deeper in the store tunnel and places three combat knives on the table in the living quarters. "These are the only weapons I can find."

"Perhaps no one expected us to be in danger," I suggest.

"According to Chris's theory they did."

"Perhaps they didn't think violence would be the answer," Chris opines priggishly.

"There's a supply of binoculars, survival kits, solar torches and personal comcens in the store tunnel," Doug says, ignoring Chris.

"I think we should use a different exit this time," I say, to give them something else to think about.

There are sealed packs of food concentrate, but Fiona has made us sandwiches from the salad and fungus stuff growing in the hydroponic unit. She reminds me of one of Chaplin's silent heroines: fey, wet and fainting. Still, it's kept her out of mischief.

We test our keywords before exiting. The weather's changed since I put my nose outside earlier and it's raining. We pull up hoods and stand listening. The summer drizzle has imposed a silence on the world. There's still no sign of yesterday's killers.

We're on an outcrop of rock. No telltale tracks leading to the entrance, I note. Someone after my own heart designed this. We have exited through an old quarry tunnel, yet now that it's closed you think you're looking at virgin rock. There are other tunnels in the hillside at intervals, plain to see, but they're all collapsed. "Deliberate," Doug says, following my glance.

Covering the hill above is an impenetrable

growth of bushes. Chris knows about such things and does not recognize the variety. It bears thorns like toughened steel.

"It's like Sleeping Beauty's magic forest," Fiona simpers. What *is* the matter with her? According to Chris, she's in shock. She's built a defensive wall because she can't handle what's happened to Ralf.

"If we could penetrate it," Doug says, "I bet we'd find the quarry crater roofed over with self-maintaining solar panels to provide power for the Base."

"A mutant variety of thorn specially grown for defence?" Chris muses.

"We'd better synchronize the time on our comcens," I suggest. "They seem to be charged up." They're solar-powered, of course. "Maths function's working."

"The phone won't be," Doug predicts. "I can't see those peasants keeping a system of booster stations or satellites working."

"There's a compass function that will be useful," Chris says, "and global positioning satellites might still be working. They were solar-powered."

"They will have drifted out of position in fifty years," Doug is happy to inform him.

I start to get the feeling that these two irritate each other. "We'd better get moving."

On this side of the Base there's no open heathland. The rocks drop into endless woods and disappear. There's nothing to be seen but billowing treetops starting a few metres below our feet.

"It's like being on a plane," Fiona exclaims, "but the clouds are green instead of snowy."

An army could be hidden within a scythe's length of us. I shrug and decide to follow a stream which runs out of the thorn bushes.

"That stream goes in the opposite direction to the way we went yesterday." I feel confident. "Note where the entrance is. Ten metres to the left of that collapsed tunnel. The triangular rock between those two oblongish ones."

I take the lead and we wade down the middle of the stream. Either side of us the trees are linked together by a near impassable net of creepers and brambles. Our boots are sealed to our trousers and everything is waterproofed.

I call a halt after twenty minutes. I don't want us to become careless with fatigue and there's not going to be any of yesterday's blundering about. We see our first man-made object after our second stop.

Chris is walking behind me. "Over to the right," he says quietly. I hold up a hand and we halt again.

An unnatural, squarish shape is discernible through the trees.

"I'll take a look," Doug says, and peels off his pack. He slides away through the undergrowth. The rest of us crouch on the bank of the stream. Fiona's eyes follow him without blinking, as though she'll be safe as long as she doesn't lose sight of him. But he disappears in a few seconds. I watch her in order to see the strain.

Ten minutes later Doug re-enters the water, twenty metres downstream. I kick myself for not having spread us out to keep watch. He did that deliberately. Sly peasant again.

"It's the remains of a house," he reports. "Burnt out years ago. No roof. There's a car in the garage which looks as though it's been battered all over with hammers." He laughs, rather artificially. The car seems to have unnerved him.

We come across more houses, all burnt out. In places where debris has dammed the stream, the swamp has entered them. We push through to the further side of one of the ruins and find what used to be a road. But it's overlaid with a carpet of vegetation, fallen trees and brambles.

Doug hacks at the mat of debris with his heel and tears up a chunk. "Covered almost to ankle depth here."

We return to our stream, since the going is easier, and quite suddenly stumble out of the trees. The clouds have cleared and after the leaf-filtered light the sun stuns us.

At chest height in front of us is the arch of a stone bridge and a road leading to a town. We climb on to its turf-covered surface. The seed-bearing stems are knee-high and undisturbed. Ahead of us are houses which have not been burnt but are obviously deserted: roofs fallen in, doors missing. I don't hesitate to advance.

There's a fallen sign leaning against a wall.

"Swanawic," Doug reads. "Hand-painted. Does that mean the house or the town?"

"Town," I say. "Name rings a bell, but there's something odd about it."

I can't think what, but why should I? We don't know the area and we were driven to the Base once only. A real initiative test. Ralf failed.

Doug kicks a lump of turf off the road surface. "Only half the thickness of the layer on the other road. So only abandoned half as long?"

"Assuming that debris accumulates at a uniform rate," Chris says prissily. "Doesn't tell us how long though."

"No," I agree. "But it looks as though the area was abandoned gradually."

"Or died over a longish period," Doug says, almost to himself.

We walk in silence like trespassers and gradually become aware of a sound like the breathing of a sleeping giant. The hairs on the back of my neck prickle.

"The seaside!" Fiona exclaims, irritating me by being right.

"Yes." Doug lets out his breath and laughs. He squeezes Fiona's hand.

The road leads towards the sound. Vegetation becomes more sparse and ancient walls support drifts of sand. The grass in the road becomes waxen. We top a slight rise and in front of us is a crescent bay, a rocky point and a windswept headland bare of trees. The waves are breaking on the beach.

It's really bizarre and somehow as big a shock as what happened to Ralf, because it's all so normal. Until we turn our backs on the sea and look at the buildings; then it's like a ruined picture postcard. The promenade is buried under shingle, the arcade a refuge for crabs.

"If we get up on that headland," Doug says, "we can use our binoculars and save a lot of legwork." Helpful when it's obvious. His heavy brown hair, cowlike eyes and sallow skin make him appear bovine and harmless. (But it's all a disguise.)

An hour and a half later we're on the highest point but all that's visible on the other side of the headland is forest, swamp, a great empty inlet from the sea and, on its further shore, the jagged ruins of a deserted city grinning at us like a gap-toothed hag.

Civilization has vanished. Except to the north-east, where a curl of smoke can be seen. As yesterday. Where Ralf died. *Civilization.*

"That," I decide, "is the direction we have to take tomorrow."

We trudge back to the Base in silence.

# *SECOND ENCOUNTER*

The next day we head towards the source of the smoke. My muscles ache from the previous day's exertions, but we've got to know what sort of world we've landed up in.

We make a detour round the place where Ralf was murdered, telling each other that we're just being cautious. It's not that we don't want to see that patch of field again. Of course not.

When we reach the edge of the forest we halt. A swathe of fields separates us from a town. I make a slow sweep with my binoculars while the rest stay well back in the trees. "It's got a wall round it," I report.

"What has?" Chris asks.

"The bloody town," I snap. "It's a walled town, like in history." Nothing fits into a recognizable pattern.

"The disease killed so many people society broke down," Chris suggests. "All strangers represent danger."

"Sounds plausible." I shrug. "But then anything does when you go to sleep in the twenty-first century and wake up in the Middle Ages."

"Shall we have our picnic?" Fiona asks, smiling serenely.

We eat tomato and pieces of fungus-like growth which serve as bread. "The hydroponic unit must have been activated at least two months before we were revived," Doug remarks unemotionally. He's the exact opposite of Fiona. She's all emotion; he's superior calm, enjoying a private joke all the time. They deserve each other.

After a rest we start to work our way along the edge of the trees towards the town. A hammering, metal on stone, gradually grows louder. The noise masks the sound of our approach, which only needs a fanfare to make it any more obvious.

Chris, Doug and I take off our packs and leave them with Fiona, hidden in the trees. I wonder about suggesting that we tie her to a tree and gag her. I just know that sooner or later she's going to do something suicidal.

We crawl forward, brushing sticks and leaves aside with our hands. The memory of Ralf possesses us.

We reach the edge of the cover, gently part a dense curtain of waist-high grass and find ourselves at the side of a road. There are three men and one woman to our right. The one who is obviously in charge has a sword at his side and is leaning on a staff looking vacantly towards the town. He wears a coarsely woven shirt under a leather jerkin, and trousers bound into gaiters above crude, leather ankle-boots. His clothes are green, but unevenly dyed. They suggest a uniform.

The others are working on the road. One man's using a pickaxe to prise out lumps of the decaying tarred surface, which he throws into the trees. The woman is setting cobblestones in rows to make a new surface. The last of the three has his back against a tree and is apparently shaping cobbles with a hammer. They're dressed in rags and have their ankles hobbled by heavy chains so that they can do no more than shuffle along.

Doug signals that he is going to approach the one with his back to the tree. I give him the nod. Chris frowns.

It takes him five minutes to work his way silently to a position behind the tree, where he's hidden by a lattice of grasses, poppies and ragwort. I see him grin to himself.

"Don't stop working. Nod if you can hear me."

The man nods.

"Who are you?" Doug asks.

"Darwin," the man answers between hammer blows.

"Why are you chained?"

"I'm an Industrial. Who are you that you don't know?"

"What's an Industrial?"

The question seems to surprise the man. His

hammering stops, then he collects himself and recommences.

"Who are you?" the man repeats.

Doug ignores his question. "Are you a criminal?"

"I'm an Industrial. Same thing," Darwin snorts.

"What did you do?"

"I was caught in a food raid on the Earthers."

"Do you live in the town?"

"Only because I'm forced to. I'm an Industrial." He becomes agitated. "Where are you from?"

"Never mind. I may be a friend," Doug says to quieten him.

"Get me away and I'll see you're rewarded. I'm a scientist, I swear it."

A church bell rings from the town. The man in charge straightens up. "Come on. Move yourselves, or you'll feel my staff across your shoulders."

His prisoners shuffle off across the new-laid cobbles towards the town. Darwin looks back, trying to pierce the tangle of greenery.

When they've gone I stand and sweep the fields with my binoculars. Groups of peasants are converging on the town gate. Some carry scythes and pitchforks. There are two wagons drawn by some animal that looks a bit like a cow. Oxen, I guess. Chris is kind enough to confirm this. The last group through the gate are the three prisoners. I can see their guard impatiently using his staff on them.

# *THE MESSAGE*

Day 4 and I wake up before the simulated-day illumination comes on. I've missed something. That's what's nagging at me.

It's tough not having Dad around, he's always been useful to take my frustrations out on. I kick him a few times, he goes sentimental and I get a shot of adrenalin, after which my thoughts go into turbo-drive. Without him I'll have to work it out on my own.

The answer lies in something we've done since we were revived. I feel it. But we went over everything last night when we returned. A walled town – prisoners like slaves – Earthers – Industrials – a scientist. Meaningless. In one giggling brainstorming session we suggested we'd been transported to another planet; we'd slept a *thousand* and fifty years; we were guinea pigs in a University disorientation experiment.

Nothing fits what we've seen.

So I start day 4 telling myself, order and analyse. Shades of McKay. Go through every tiny event from showering to sleeping and find the key.

I am determined to find it myself, whatever it is. Otherwise Doug or Chris might, then they'd have the advantage. I discount Fiddle-de-dee; that would be too humiliating.

I start to recite yesterday's events and find myself drifting back into a warm, dozing state. I unseal my sleepsac and push my feet hard against the plastic coating on the wall. I feel rock through the insulating cocoon of bubbles.

I'm underground. Brings to mind my Welsh mining ancestors. Short, dark, devious. Suspicious of anyone who might try to manipulate them. Me.

Begin again. Right after Ralf. Day 2. We went out. Decided to go southwest. No. Start at the beginning. I get up. Shower. Clean clothes from the stores. Breakfast. Tidy the living quarters. Discussion. Decide to explore. Preparations: weapons, food, comcens, camcorder—

Shit! I jerk upright. That's it! The stupidity! We've never stopped running since we woke up. First after Ralf. Then, in a state of shock, after explanations.

I pull on my dirty clothes, hopping about, furious with myself. While all the time it's been there waiting. If I thought of leaving a message for the next group to wake, then it's a dead cert that whoever put the Base together left one for us.

In order to be sure I'm thinking clearly, I force

myself to slow down and have a high energy biscuit before going to the main control room. We looked in there but touched nothing for fear of disrupting the Base's functioning. Stupid again. There'll be checks and warnings and automatic overrides against idiots.

There are three swivel chairs on rollers. I seat myself central to a large control screen. A console faces me. Voice or manual operation. I choose manual.

Whoever arranged for me to wake first would have made sure I could access information. I type "Any messages?" just as I used to on the home computer when everyone was out. The screen above the keyboard glows into life.

A face materializes.

Staring out at me is my grandfather. No! Unbelievable. My *father*. Aged, strained, tired...

I press *pause*.

Less than a week for me, but time didn't stop for him. I knew it, theoretically. But here's the reality and what do I feel? The same as usual with Dad – angry! How dare he surprise me by getting older without me realizing.

How long since he recorded this? How old was he then? How old is he now?

I still don't believe he's dead. He's going to tell me where to find him.

I restart the message.

"Hallo, Cindy."

Interesting that. I never thought of voices ageing.

"Do you know, I've gone back to thinking of you as Lucy again."

Of course I don't know, but it's typical.

"How many times have I looked at you in your capsule and longed to wake you and hold you again, like when you were a little girl. All the Hibernation Programme parents who were allowed a video-view of their children when things collapsed suffered the same agony of desire for contact, but denied themselves. They had one last sight, then went to face the future without knowing the location of the Base. They'd agreed to that for the sake of security. But the pain of that self-sacrifice was made worse by never being certain that they were doing the right thing.

"I was more fortunate. The Vice Chancellor appointed me Base Guardian. That was twenty years ago. Since then I've watched over all of you, and agonized over my decision to allow you to hibernate. I'll not survive to know whether I did the right thing." He pauses. "This message is to warn you. I've very little time. They've got Suzie."

My little sister. Seven plus twenty. Who's got her?

"You remember the disease? Yes, of course you do. It was yesterday, as far as you're concerned. The Mexico Virus. Was it called that when you took the sleep?"

Stop waffling. Who's got Suzie?

"The University virologists calculated that, with luck, it would take four years to produce a vaccine. It was halfway through those years that we decided to offer you the sleep. We used the suspended animation part of the Space Research Programme to isolate you. You were to remain in hibernation until the disease was defeated. Five years at the most. All unofficial, of course. The Government didn't know where its money was going.

"You'll know by now that our plans changed. The world was on the point of developing a vaccine when the riots came."

I *pause* for a quick calculation. That would be when the second wave of sleepers went into hibernation.

"It was the animal protectionists who destroyed the research programme. They took away infected animals, some with a new strain of the virus, and the fresh outbreak of the disease which followed gave the final push towards the Collapse.

"The other betrayer of humanity was the Pure Earth Party. It relied on ignorance and media hype of every news item which denigrated science, from processed food to nuclear energy.

"SSUs – Self-supporting Units – were established with Wardens to govern them. Central government devolved to the regions. Ranger groups were formed to keep movement to a minimum. Horses replaced machines. Pollution became a major crime.

"Am I making much sense, Lucy?"

Cindy.

"My mind's on Suzie. But I'll come to your situation. The Vice Chancellor's committee selected those who should take the sleep. You are all children of University staff and are all fifteen or sixteen. No one older could hibernate because of the danger of calcification of the joints. They didn't take anyone younger because it was thought they'd not be mature enough to cope with the shock.

"That's what the tests were for. Everyone had to be adaptable, physically fit and well-balanced."

So why us?

"Your mother used her influence with the Vice Chancellor to get you on the programme even though your results were only marginal. I don't know how she managed it, but you have her to thank for your survival.

"She disappeared during the riots. A lot of people did."

I wonder what the euphemism "disappeared" conceals and feel a flicker of unease.

"I must be quick.

"Your brother no longer calls himself Matthew. He is known as Brother Soil. I'm so used to it that it sounds normal. He's a cross between a monk and a state security policeman. To start with he worked for the Resistance but from what I hear he has gone over to the other side. I think he's been responsible for the death of at least two resisters. He knew about the Hibernation Programme, but not the whereabouts of the Base. That was a closely guarded secret and we've never been disturbed here.

"Listen. If the Base malfunctions you will automatically be resuscitated. If that happens before society is back to normal, take extreme care. Don't let anyone know that you're from the Age of Technology. Only those who survived the disease are judged pollution-free. It would be a death sentence if anyone found out how you survived. Believe me, it's true. You must believe me."

I do. So does Ralf.

"I've arranged a contact with the Resistance for you. You're about three miles southeast of a small town now called Werham. Most places reverted to ancient names. You must contact a Master Fern. He will help you. Or his son will. He'll pass on the duty. Life expectancy is dropping.

"You must say that you are his kin from Sarum. That's your password. 'Kin from Sarum.'

"I must go. It's evening. Lucy, your sister is to be executed tomorrow. She was caught using a radio, trying to keep in contact with other resisters. I must try to rescue her. If this message awaits you when you wake, you may assume that I failed. She needs me more than you do. What they do to resisters is not pleasant."

I remember Ralf and feel another touch of queasiness. I'll never know what happened to Suzie. Or Dad. Thirty years ago. So whatever it was has long ceased.

"I've done my duty and watched over you for twenty years. My love to you, my timeless Lucy. I hope we really did the best for you."

There's no answer to that one.

* * *

That night I lie awake. We've all watched Dad's message several times and gutted it for clues.

But that's not what's stopping me sleeping. The real reason is that of the three people I've been landed with in this retarded hell-hole, the only one whose behaviour I'm confident I can predict is music-in-the-head Fiona. And all I can say about her is that she'll do something that will pitchfork us into a low-tech mincing machine if she's not kept on a short leash with a choke collar.

In a way, though, Fiona is more normal than the rest of us. The shock of the death of everyone she knew tipped her over the edge. While all I feel is anger at Dad for getting himself killed, if that's what he did. And after the first shock of hearing about Suzie, I find that she's become unreal: how could someone of twenty-seven be my little sister? As for Matthew, I never got on with him. He saw through me; and anyone who changes his name to Brother Soil is not living on the same planet as me. And Mum? The more I think about her "disappearing" the more suspicious I feel. If there was chaos, she'd survive, never mind what Dad assumed; and if I'd been her I'd have dumped him as a liability a.s.a.p. I quite believe she could walk in anytime, saying, "What's kept you so long?"

That's me and Fiona, then. What about Doug and Chris? What makes them tick? Why aren't they grief-stricken? Are they as self-centred as me? Was being a sociopath the main quality required for admission to the Hibernation Programme?

# *THE TOWN*

Yippee! We're going to town. Shops, parties, clubs, crowds, fun, life! Alternatively, there's Werham.

Chris has sewn our fancy dress. I knew the selection procedure had some use for him. Doug's done the macho bit: crawling up to the town gates at night and planting listening devices. I've scripted our opening speeches based on what's been heard. Oh, and Fiona. She's made sandwiches and screwed up our plans. My plans!

I'd put her down to stay in the trees with Doug and film mine and Chris's approach to the town. We had miniaturized transmitters sewn into our clothes so that if something went wrong, scythe-wise, those who came after wouldn't make the same mistake.

Trash that idea. Sunk by Fiona's sweet, implacable smile, her shield against reality. She is coming with us! Are nervous breakdowns catching?

I make the ultimate sacrifice to save my plan: I have a girlie gossip with Fiona. It's like having a catheter inserted in my brain. I don't get anywhere until I have the inspiration of suggesting that we're being punished. I get through all right then, but I don't end up where I planned.

It seems she's got the idea that the sleep was a journey to her father, who's waiting for her someplace, which might be Werham. She has to find him before someone called Robin, her stepfather as far as I can tell, catches up with her. This Robin is into groping her in her mother's absence, and Fiona mère is as impermeable to enlightenment in this matter as daughter is to the advantages, survival-wise, of staying behind with Doug. I get out of the swamp that is Fiona's psyche, but with my plans sunk.

We end up approaching the town late one afternoon, with girls a regulation three paces behind. Added to that indignity, we are the pack animals and have to hump the bundles we've put together in the interests of authenticity.

Doug and Chris are armed with staffs. By the way he handles his, I can tell that Doug would like to crack a few skulls. He's also got a ferocious commando knife strapped to his forearm. I have a smaller one, but Chris baulked at this.

We pass through the town gates, which are open and leaning against the nearby buildings because the hinges are half rusted through. That sets the tone for the place.

"What a dump," Doug mutters.

There are shops each side of the main street but they're mixed in with houses. A butcher's has lambs tethered outside; a carpenter's opens into a front room; a fishmonger's has fish swimming in an old water tank from somebody's attic; a junk shop sells used nails and plates which would have been new two weeks ago, my time. House windows whose glass has broken have rags and wooden shutters. Roofs are changing from tile to thatch.

"This is even worse than we expected," Chris says. "The church is still standing," he adds, seeing a tower between two roofs.

"That's all right then," I say.

The few people about stare at us because we're strangers, not because we're from the Age of Technology.

"Quality of their clothes is poor," Doug comments.

"They're all shorter than us," I say in surprise.

"Poor diet," Chris suggests. "We're too clean."

Our clothes are appropriate but the quality's too good. Women dress in long skirts, shapeless blouses fastened with laces, and shawls. Men wear smocks that hang like tents over thick, baggy trousers which are tucked into leather boots. As much fashion sense as McKay and his colleagues.

"We're back in the Middle Ages," Doug mutters.

Ahead of us is the open space of a crossroads with horse-trough, pump and stocks. Everything your medieval peasant needs for a quality life experience. A man is sitting on the edge of the horse-trough aimlessly banging his heel against the stone.

"Try him," I tell Chris.

We stand back, prepared to flee.

"Greetings, friend. May your land be fruitful." That's our prepared opening.

The man looks startled and Chris has a try at what I think he believes is a reassuring smile. It must be like staring death in the face.

"Ock," the man says. He gives the impression of trying to tie a knot in his neck, then repeats, "Ock, ock, ock" in case we didn't catch it first time. In spite of these efforts no words are forthcoming.

"Bloody great," Doug says through clenched teeth. "We've picked on the village idiot." He shifts the staff in his hands.

Chris ploughs on as if everything is as expected. "We seek the house of Master Fern."

The man glances about as though looking for an escape route. Chris does not seem surprised by the effect he's having. Perhaps it's the normal reaction to him.

I'm just wondering, what now? when Fiona decides to make her contribution. I feel my stomach tighten. I'd like to clamp the wispy twat in the stocks.

She steps up to the man, smiles radiantly as only a model or someone living in a private world can, and lays a hand on his head. Her shawl slips back and her blonde hair billows out in the slight breeze like a halo. In these surroundings it seems to gleam. I try not to notice the effect she's having on the one or two spectators nearby, who are ignorant of the benefits of shampoo and animal testing.

"Do not be afraid," she tells the man. "All will be well now that we are here."

The man gazes at her adoringly. I see Chris digging his nails into his palms. What's bugging him is not the danger, but Fiona's departure from the script.

"My friends call me Fiona," she tells the man. "You are my friend, aren't you?"

The man's head trembles.

"We seek another who is our friend. Master Fern. Can you tell us where he lives?"

The man points. "Eas-Eas ... East Street," he stammers.

She allows her hand to drift from his head. "Remember, you are not to fear."

Fiona sets off in the direction the man has indicated and we follow her, trying not to see what's happening behind us. The shops and houses in this street are in better repair. Above a door hangs a sign showing a posy of herbs between two fern fronds. The word "Herbalist" has all but peeled off, but the picture tells anyone interested that this is Master Fern's shop. I realize with a shock what this implies: people here are illiterate.

Fiona smiles.

# *THE HERBALIST*

"Be unobtrusive," I told them before we left the Base. "Our Resistance contact won't thank us if we arrive with a pitchfork-wielding mob in tow."

Perhaps Fiddles doesn't know the word unobtrusive.

As we approach Master Fern's shop I give in to the urge to take a quick look back up the street. The village idiot is still gawping after us and has been joined by a group of his peers, who are drooling in support.

"Bloody, bloody, bloody," I mutter. I decide that I'm in favour of compulsory euthanasia.

Chris lifts a latch and the shop door strikes a bell hanging above it like a booby-trap. From a doorway in the rear a man scuttles forward into the gloom of the shop.

"Good-day to you, strangers," he says, wringing his hands and half bowing. His voice is nasally sharp. There is something tortoise-like about his balding head and stretched neck. He wears a shirt under a jerkin, trousers and shoes. They're all of better quality than the clothes we've seen so far.

Chris waits for his eyes to adjust before speaking. Good self-control, I have to admit.

"Greetings, Master Fern," he begins. "You are Master Fern?"

"Such is my privilege. Whom have I the honour of addressing?"

"We are your kin from Sarum."

There is silence.

Master Fern looks about sixty. Grey-haired, suspicious, obstinate. Could he be the man Dad knew? He'd have been thirty at the time of the message. Suddenly I know that he's going to deny having kin in Sarum. Fiona's smiling benignly.

"I have no kin in Sarum." Bingo!

"Our journey has been long and the message is old."

Chris is ad-libbing but he's still in character. Now I think of it, if you dressed Chris in Fern's clothes they could swop places and no one would ever know the difference. I was right to nominate him as spokesman. Doug would have given Fern a couple of cracks round the head to refresh his memory. I can feel his suppressed rage at the town. I'd like to know what offends him.

Master Fern jerks back in surprise. "What are you telling me?"

"Were you not expecting us?"

Master Fern shakes his head slowly, horrified by

what has manifested itself in his shop.

"But you *are* the Master Fern we seek?" Chris pursues. "There is no other?"

Master Fern swallows. "I am the only one."

"A message was left with you to expect us, was it not?" Chris persists.

"With my father," Master Fern whispers. "He told me." He looks round his shop as though the pottery jars with plant names are unfamiliar.

I remember Dad saying that life expectancy was dropping. If Master Fern is the son, he can't be much more than forty; nowhere near sixty.

"Master Fern," Fiona says, stepping up to the counter, "we shall stay with you. Have no fear. The time of waiting is over."

God knows what she's on about. Waiting for her father?

Master Fern stares at her fair hair, which even in the gloom seems to radiate light. He gestures to a hatch in the counter. She leads the way as graciously as royalty receiving the freedom of a city, and we file along a passage into a back room.

There's a scrubbed wooden table, upright chairs, a dresser and a stone floor. All the pictures on the walls are faded prints of landscapes. Sad. Through the window I see a garden crammed with vegetables.

Master Fern shouts a name through another door and a girl, apparently our age, comes in wiping her hands on her apron.

"This is my daughter, Willow," Master Fern

says, without looking at her. "These travellers are our guests. Where's Pansy? Tell the girl to fetch sustenance."

Chris watches the girl collect a jug and plates from the dresser. She's as tall as her father, dark-haired, solidly built, though her name is appropriate because her eyes are a silver-green like willow leaves and her movements are supple.

I note that she keeps her eyes down. Browbeaten?

When she's gone, Master Fern says, "Willow knows nothing of this. She would not understand."

"Are there others who wait for kin from Sarum?" Doug asks.

The stronger light makes Master Fern look shabbier than in the shop. A desiccated bundle of herbs. "In my father's time there were. Perhaps they passed on the duty. Many who lived through the Judgement were polluted by old ways of thinking."

"The Judgement?" Doug demands.

"When mankind was punished for the sins of the Age of Technology."

"The Collapse," I exclaim, making the connection.

"That is what my father called it." Master Fern looks suddenly agitated. "If the Rangers heard of you using that word they would think you were an Industrial."

"We saw some Industrials working on the road," Chris says soothingly.

"Misguided creatures. They follow the old ways. The Rangers hunt them down if their numbers become too great."

"One said he was a scientist," Chris prompts.

Master Fern suddenly seems to realize what he is explaining. "Who are you? Where are you from?"

"We are strangers, not Industrials," Chris reassures him. "Do you not welcome strangers? We hear that one was killed near here recently."

"That one brought a machine on to the land."

Does he mean Ralf's camera?

Master Fern notices our frowns and snaps: "Pollution. The crops would have failed if the blood-price had not been paid."

"Are all machines bad?" I ask.

"Yes," he says, "though some would debate it." His eyes dart from one to another of us. We've tried to make ourselves indistinguishable from the people of Werham, but it's easy to see we're different. "Where are you from?" he repeats. "There were stories of people from before the Judgement who withdrew to a land beneath the earth and would one day arise."

Chris nods. "We heard such a story."

"It is not possible." Master Fern jumps to his feet. "Do you say you are from before the Judgement? A world ruled by scientists?" His horror is like a slap.

Just then Willow returns with a younger girl. She is a half-starved, red-jointed skivvy with sores round her mouth. Pansy, presumably. They set two trays on the table and place pottery and wooden mugs in front of us. I get a wooden one. Willow pours beer while Pansy puts bread, cheese and onions on the table.

"Knives, girl," Master Fern barks at Pansy.

"I'll fetch them," Willow tells her. "You take the trays." Pansy scurries out and I have the impression that Willow rules domestic affairs.

"Is there anyone alive from before the Judgement?" I ask.

"You are forward, missie," Master Fern informs me. He seems affronted at being cross-examined by a girl in front of his daughter.

Willow places knives on the table, then turns as if to go out the door, but instead steps sideways so that she is half-hidden by the dresser.

Master Fern clears his throat. "There are still a few, but the Rangers watch them. If they speak out of turn," he looks at me, "they are returned to the soil."

I don't bother to ask what that means.

He seems to reach a decision. "You may rest here for one night. I allow this because of my father's promise, but guard your tongues. You put my household in danger. You understand, I think only of Willow."

"Thank you, Father," Willow says from behind him. Fern jumps and his face twitches irritably.

"We are deeply grateful for your hospitality," Chris says quickly, "and if we can repay you in any way, we shall be glad to."

I take a swig of beer. I don't usually like it but it's sweet and goes well with the cheese and rough bread. As I drink, the wooden lip of my mug goes slimy and I think that I can feel other wet mouths that have slobbered on it. I have a sudden longing for dishwashers.

"Who rules this town?" Doug asks.

"The Warden with the advice of the Council." Master Fern's voice becomes weighty. "I expect to be on the Council next year. As herbalist, I have a certain standing in the town."

"Being related to Squire Widgeon is a help too," Willow puts in.

I take another gulp to hide my expression. "Who rules the country as a whole?"

"There are High Wardens of each region. Ours sits in Sarum, which is the chief city of Wessex. They meet twice a year to decide large matters."

"In London?" Chris asks.

Master Fern gathers his jerkin in his hands. "London was the source of pollution. Judgement fell heaviest there. The sink was emptied and cleansed."

It sounds like a litany.

Master Fern flicks his fingers at Willow to clear the table. I offer to help. Any longer in his presence and I'll unscrew his lizard-like trachea. Let him try flicking his fingers at me.

First thing I do when I've dumped the plates in the kitchen is pay a visit to the loo, which turns out to be a hole in the ground in a fly-blown hut halfway down the garden. Leaves serve as toilet tissue; I kid you not. After this experience, I decide that I do not intend to spend the rest of my life in this particular microsecond of eternity. I've got one life and it's going to be spent in the twenty-first century, even if it means kicking everyone else out of the Base and setting up my own SSU. Enough videos there to keep me occupied for a few years, and I prefer a screen between me and film sets like this.

Willow's in the kitchen washing up in a sort of witch's cauldron. She's shaving flakes off a dirty grey lump of something which just might be soap. Hot water to replenish the cauldron stands in an iron pot on a blackened range built into one wall. Just like the Aga at home.

"Are you all named after trees and stuff?" I ask.

"Mostly, I suppose," she says, as though it's never struck her before.

I grunt because, having established that fascinating fact, there's not much else to say.

"Where d'you get your water for cooking?" I ask next, having noticed a stream in the garden not far from the soak-away sewage system.

"We have a pump," Willow says proudly. "Us'ens scullery is built over a well."

"When did you last have the water analysed?"

My tone's patronizing and she looks at me quickly. Not the bumpkin I thought. "What's that then?" she asks.

"Just my idea of a joke." At least they don't draw from the stream, I reassure my stomach.

I follow Willow into a gloomy room off the kitchen. The serving-girl Pansy is preparing vegetables there. The window is without glass but can be closed with a wooden shutter. There's a hand pump over a sink. I try cranking it and cold, apparently clean, water gushes out.

"Willow," I ask when we're back in the kitchen, "have you ever seen an aeroplane?"

"No, I haven't, thank the Lord!" Willow exclaims. "Wicked, polluting machines, so I've heard tell. Mind you, I doubt that people really flew up in the air. You know how tales grow with the tellin'."

"Yes," I say. I'm beginning to doubt it too. "Aren't you curious about us?"

"Father don't hold with curiosity," Willow says piously. "Still, he ain't here, is he? So tell us about y'selves."

For a second I'm tempted to blast her with a list of things I've taken for granted all my life, starting with tap water and working up to orbiting factories. It would be useless. She couldn't understand and wouldn't believe. Anyway, what do I care what she believes, as long as she's no threat.

I take a different tack. "Where I come from, women are equal to men."

"Better not let my dad hear you say that," Willow giggles. "It'd give 'en a seizure."

We both laugh. She might as well think there's

some rapport possible between us. I pick up a knife with a blade the colour of lead. "Did someone in Werham make this?"

"Aye. The Council allows a blacksmith near the north gate."

"You don't sound as though you like him."

"In the opinion of decent folks," Willow says, sounding like her father, "a smith is first cousin to an Industrial."

"Did the blacksmith make your water pump?"

"No. That comes from a travelling tinker. He does trade with the Industrials for such things."

I nod. "Isn't the pump a machine?"

"Not so long as it do save I carrying water from the stream."

Self-interest still rules, I'm happy to see.

"Tell us about that boy with the fair hair," Willow says, giving me a knowing glance. "Are you or the other girl sweet on 'en?"

"Chris," I tell her. "But call him Christopher if you want to make a good impression. Not my sort. Why, d'you fancy him?"

"I might. Then again, I might not. But I do know when a boy fancies I."

We laugh. All girls together. How jolly. Human nature doesn't change, does it? I'll be able to operate here as effectively as ever. And willow bends, doesn't it?

# *PLANS*

It's like something out of one of those old children's adventures.The four chums meet by candlelight – but innocently: oh, so innocently – in the boys' bedroom to plan their holiday adventures. They feel that this year something really exciting will happen.

"Where do we go from here?" I ask, automatically appointing myself chair.

We're in the large bedroom over Master Fern's shop. The furniture was antique fifty years ago. There's a brass bedstead, double, a wardrobe with a long mottled mirror and a table used as a washstand. Bleached wallpaper curls arthritically at the edges. Why this room is kept empty while Willow sleeps in the attic was not explained.

The bathroom next door has turned into a junk room.

Doug has examined the central heating and declared, "Even without electric pumps they could have a gravity feed system."

Perhaps we could set up as plumbers.

"It's happened before," Chris informs us. "Barbarians living among the ruins of Rome."

We can hear Master Fern sleeping wheezingly in the room across the landing.

What the four chums want are some jolly exciting ideas. Chris starts the ball rolling. "The first thing to decide is what we've been sent here to achieve."

Being led by event seems to offend him.

"We weren't sent to achieve anything," I point out. "Things were supposed to be back to normal when we woke up, ready for us to get on with our lives."

"If what the message said was true," Doug murmurs.

"What d'you mean?"

"Those who controlled the Hibernation Programme might have had a different agenda to our parents."

"Whatever anyone's agenda was, what we've got to do is remake the twenty-first century," I say. I'm not having any argument on that point.

Amazingly, neither Chris nor Doug looks as though he feels the same inescapable imperative. Fiona's patient smile says that she's living in her own private century already.

"The next batch of sleepers awakes in four months," I remind them, but find myself thinking that the timings can be reset. "As I see it we've got three choices. One, we can set up our own community centred on the Base."

"How long could that survive, even with the resources of the Base?" Doug asks. "We'd have to expand or die. Then we'd clash with this society."

"I agree," I say quickly. "Or, two, we can join this society and try to change it from within. I take it we don't want to live in a medieval slum?"

The idea seems to amuse Doug.

"Don't forget Ralf," Chris says. "These people are hostile to anything technological."

"Can you see fifty sleepers being allowed to set up house in this town?" Doug laughs.

"There might be other towns which are not so reactionary," I suggest, pushing the point so that they end up where I want them.

"Not from what we've been told," Chris says stiffly. "We'd have to become indistinguishable from the Earthers in order to survive."

"The third possibility is the Industrials. Could we join them?" I ask, coming to what I see as our only hope of re-creating a decent standard of living.

"From what Master Fern said when you were in the kitchen," Chris tells me, "the Industrials are nothing more than gypsies. The only industrial thing about them is their name."

"Fern may be prejudiced," Doug says, smiling.

I'd like to know what his private joke is.

"They make water pumps," I add. "That means they can cast metal, doesn't it?"

"There is a fourth possibility," Doug goes on. "We and the rest of the sleepers could take over a town by force. Train the people. Make them technological."

"We've no weapons," Chris objects.

"Make them."

"How many of the sleepers would be willing to do that?" I ask. "Besides, I can't see the Wardens and Rangers allowing us to take over one of their towns."

"Just an idea," Doug shrugs, unconcerned.

I feel a draught across my back and draw my shawl closer. The candle flame flickers and shadows distort expressions so that I can't tell what anyone's really thinking.

"We need to contact the Industrials in order to get information, if nothing else," I say, bringing them back to where I want to be.

"How do we do that?" Chris asks.

"Not that difficult," Doug tells him helpfully. "This town possesses three Industrials looked after by one guard. All I have to do is set them free and let them introduce me to their people."

There's a pause, pregnant with calculation by Chris and me.

"On your own, do you mean?" I ask.

"That would be easiest."

"No," I say. To let him go off would mean I'd lose control. "You must have back-up." Best I can think of just now.

"I want to spend some time investigating the

social system in this town," Chris says, disqualifying himself.

"I'll go with Doug," I say.

"What about Fiona?" Chris asks.

Doug reaches out and turns her face towards him. "You'll stay with Chris," he tells her.

Fiona smiles with irritating calm. "You must go to the Industrials. I see now what has to be done. There must be no divisions."

I feel a chill again.

"I need to go to the Base for some equipment before I tackle the guard," Doug says. "I'll collect two radios so that we can keep in contact."

I nod. "There's a burnt-out house in the woods near where the Industrials were working on the road. Doug and I could leave the radio there for you to pick up," I tell Chris.

"We must have proper call times and listen each day," Chris says. He proposes a list of words as code in case of danger. Doug grunts his agreement. I get the feeling only half his mind is on this.

"It would be best if I left now," Doug announces. "Then I could grab a few hours' sleep at the Base." He turns to me. "I'll meet you at midday at the place by the road where we hid to watch the Industrials. Travelling at night in those clothes would be impossible."

I can't think of any reason to object, but my stomach churns suspiciously.

"Sounds like a good idea," Chris says.

He'd agree to anything if it meant getting rid of

Doug, and if I were Doug I'd be glad to avoid sharing a bed with Chris.

"How are you going to get out of town?" I ask. "Willow told me there was a Watch."

Doug pushes aside the tattered curtain. It's a clear night with a moon. "I'll wade along the stream at the end of the garden until I reach the town wall. That will be easy enough to climb."

"Your feet will get wet," Chris says. I can see him regret it as soon as he's spoken.

Doug laughs patronizingly. "We're going to have to get used to being wet in this world."

He's evidently looking forward to that. Outward Bound type. "I don't intend to get used to anything here," I say.

I go downstairs with Doug to let him out. "Remember Ralf," I say.

"I've not forgotten," he says as he stands outside the back door. The night seems to make him want to exchange confidences. "This isn't a medieval town, you know. It's the decadent remnants of our society. These people are jackals living on our leftovers. I'd suffocate here. Chris can investigate for as long as he likes. In the end he'll forget what he's looking for and become one of them."

"See you about midday," I say.

He strides off into the moonlight, a broad, powerful figure armed with a staff. I hope, for the Watch's sake, that they don't run into each other.

For some reason I remember a working model

of a Victorian paddle-steamer Doug built. It had been pictured in the local paper and put in a museum.

I lock the door and creep up to the attic that Fiona and I share with Willow. I try to make myself comfortable on a mattress which is stuffed with straw or hay or some other bucolic rubbish. Every time I change position I have to hammer all the stalks blunt.

This is no holiday adventure.

# *LOSING CONTROL*

Breakfast is a revolting porridge-like pigswill. Master Fern spoons honey on to sweeten it and slurps. I eat it using the not-breathing-through-the-nose technique. I developed this method when little to enable me to swallow undercooked eggs with whites like warm mucus, until I discovered that throwing them against the wall circumvented the whole process.

Chris, Fern-like, eats with relish: the mush has been prepared by Willow's fair hand. The morning light seems to bleach the colour out of him, so that he is as pale as a corpse.

Fiona eats daintily with an appreciative smile. Willow does not eat with us. She knows her place. These are the good old days.

I grimace at Chris. He doesn't respond; unctuously never stepping out of character. The trouble with living in a solipsistic universe is that other people are no more than zoo specimens. What I liked about Ralf was that he broke out of his cage and joined me.

"Our companion of the road left early," Chris tells Master Fern.

"So I was told. And you?" Master Fern speaks through slurps.

"Cindy will leave this morning."

"Will it look strange, a girl walking out of town alone?" I ask him.

He purses his lips judiciously. "Not as long as you are not seen to stray beyond the fields." He studies me. "Call yourself Cinnamon."

I nod, trying to remember what cinnamon tastes like. I think I'd rather be Cayenne.

Master Fern looks speculatively at Chris.

Chris forestalls him. "Salt. I'll stay if I may."

Master Fern's eyes narrow. "Very well. Apprentice Salt. Son of my cousin Dogwood in Sarum. You are here to learn the herbalist's arts. Until we find you are unsuitable."

I wonder what's changed since last night, then I notice Willow smirking in the doorway and reassess who really runs this household.

Master Fern makes no suggestion about Fiona, only glancing at her and nodding.

Can we trust him? I wonder. Only until he gets scared is the answer. Be useful to have a lever on him. I wonder what vices the little shit's got.

Later, I say a fond farewell to Chris by reminding him where he can pick up the radio and the times for transmission. I don't plan to let one half of the operation drift while I'm not there.

"Watch Fiona," I add. "I don't like her wooden smile."

"If she's regarded as odd, it may be an advantage. Master Fern seems to treat her cautiously." He speaks without inflexion. I get the feeling he may go hyper at any minute.

I bustle up the road like a middle-aged matron, the way they all walk. The long skirt helps. I'm relieved to find that the village idiot is not in the square. I don't know how it would go down if I tried out my self-defence lessons on him.

No one pays me any special attention. I look at cloth on a stall. Dull colours. What're aniline dyes made from? Then I notice farm tools. Thick, heavy implements. Murderous. Ralf. These people are psychopaths and we'd better not forget it.

I reach the town gate. A landscape like an old painting stretches in front of me, with peasants toiling in the fields, carts being loaded and cows, sheep and goats grazing under the eyes of swains. Hey nonny nonny. I take the newly cobbled road that skirts the woods. Somewhere further along it the Industrials are working – we hope.

I walk until I'm hidden by a rise in the neighbouring fields, then I duck into the trees. The undergrowth tears at my trailing skirt. I sigh for the snag-proof clothes I've left at the Base. At least it's not raining. After a few minutes I'm panting. There's no sound from the road but I try to move quietly by lifting branches out of my way.

I've no idea how far I've come. Where's Doug? Has he done what he was supposed to? Too many questions altogether where he's concerned. I halt and a hand is suddenly clamped over my mouth.

"Why didn't you bring a brass band?" Doug whispers in my ear.

No, he doesn't turn me on, I can confirm it. "You try walking in this fancy dress," I hiss back. "It's all right for you in your proper clothes. Why are you, anyway?" I ask, registering the military style survival outfit through the sweat in my eyes.

"Different people this time." Doug smiles. He smiles a lot in a laugh-with-me, Godfatherish way. "I'm going to be myself from now on."

"Hadn't noticed you being anything else."

Doug leads me through the trees, flattening obstacles for me, until we come to a pile of supplies from the Base.

"I haven't been to the burnt-out house yet," he tells me. "We'll free the Industrials and stop there as we get away."

"I can't see the Earthers following us far."

"The Ranger guarding the Industrials sums them up – beat someone in chains."

Doug takes a hessian-wrapped bundle from the pile: long-handled shears. We can hear the hammering from the road now. We crawl the last stretch. At one point Doug lies on brambles so that I can walk over him, like First World War infantry flattening barbed wire.

The scene is a rerun of a few days ago: the same

three Industrials and one Ranger.

Doug slides away, dragging his bundle with him. He halts behind the scientist's tree.

"Friend Darwin," he murmurs. "Do you hear me?"

The hammering does not falter.

"I hear you. Are you going to tell me who you are this time?"

"Information later," Doug says calmly. "Can you get the Ranger to come over here?"

"Why should I do that?"

"You could stay here and perish of cold and hunger in the winter."

The Industrial chuckles. "Ready?"

Doug stands up behind the tree, shears in hand. "Whenever you like."

Darwin lets out a yell, drops his hammer and rolls over hugging his hand.

The Ranger turns round angrily. "Get up, you idle bag of pollution."

Darwin moans again. Overacting, I think. The Ranger won't be taken in.

"D'you want to feel my staff across your back?"

Darwin repeats his horror movie groan. I wince.

The Ranger thwacks him across the shoulders. Darwin rolls and wraps himself round his legs.

Doug steps out and swings the shears in an arc. The Ranger hears nothing, but an instant before he's struck he instinctively hunches his shoulders. The shears skim across his shoulders and there's a sound like a mallet hitting a croquet ball.

The Ranger spirals into a heap.

The other two Industrials stand gaping.

"Get him off me," Darwin demands.

One-handed, Doug heaves the Ranger into the grass by the road where he's out of sight.

"Cindy," Doug says. "You're going to be slower than us, so you'd better get moving."

He's right. So why the uneasiness?

"I'll wait at the burnt-out house," I agree.

"Take a radio with you. I haven't been able to test them. I'll call you before we start to move."

He unsheaths the metal shears and severs one of Darwin's shackles.

I crash through the woods towards the house. It takes me longer to find than I expect. I turn on the radio and wait. There are soot stains on the walls and the jagged edges of broken bricks are eroding into sand. The world's going backwards. I wonder why Doug's taking so long to release the Industrials. Cutting one of Darwin's legs free hadn't taken more than two seconds.

The radio bleeps.

"Hallo, Cindy. Do you hear me?"

"Hear you fine. What's holding you up? Over."

"There's a change of plan. We're going in a different direction. According to Darwin the Ranger's wife brings him his dinner about now. So you'd better get back to town quick. Over and out."

"What? Doug!" I shriek uselessly at the radio. "Doug, you bastard!"

Out-manoeuvred by a peasant.

# *THE LADY FIONA*

I hide the radio under rubble in the burnt-out house. Carrying it about when three Industrials have escaped and a Ranger's brains have been scrambled is a shortcut to being skewered on a pitchfork.

By the time I've torn my way through the brambles and emerged on to the cobbles near the town, my clothes are bejewelled with burrs, snagged and stained, and sweat is trickling down my back and thighs. I stand still to regain my composure and swear a few more times at Doug. Then I laugh. He's a bastard, but the only one I've got any time for. He decides what he wants and bulldozes his way to it.

When I enter the town I find Chris, Fiona and Willow at the crossroads trying to look inconspicuous. I bustle up to them and explain the change of plan. Chris puts on a disapproving expression.

"We're on our way to gather herbs," he explains.

But that's as far as he gets because the village idiot chooses that moment to put in an appearance. He throws himself at Fiona's feet, starts kissing the hem of her dress and babbling incomprehensibly. People suddenly appear out of nowhere, like disturbed termites, and begin drifting in our direction.

"He's drawing attention to us," Chris mutters to Willow.

She grabs the man's shoulder. "What's up, Cluck?"

"The lady. Her made I t-talk," he tells Willow, without taking his eyes off Fiona. "Her freed us'ens t-tongue."

Bloody great, I think. Now we've got a miracle-worker to liven things up. It seems that miracles have side-effects just like regular drugs. Devotion, for one. We've now got an audience of half a dozen, and others are being drawn to us like iron filings to a magnet. This is the first time I've seen people move at more than funeral pace.

The shopkeepers are all happy to leave their premises unattended. There's no modern sense of discipline. What's needed is some urban dishonesty to keep people pinned down where they ought to be.

Cluck, the idiot, tells each new arrival the good news. Unselfishly I step back to allow them a better view; although, because of my dishevelled state, I'm fairly inconspicuous.

A woman with a baby pushes her way up to Fiona. "Lady, my baby has croup. Will you touch her?"

It seems they're into miracles. Fiona obliges. "Hush, little one," she murmurs. The baby appears fascinated by the golden-framed face above her and her crying changes to a contented gurgle. I wonder about charging for this service.

A man calls out, "Lady, my leg will not heal."

Chris is standing paralysed.

"Who are you, Lady?" a voice asks.

Fiona begins to speak. "I am your friend. I came to find my father. He speaks to me. He guided me here. When we are united we shall live together as one family. You are my family."

Gibberish, I think. It sounds like the stuff she was telling me the other night, mixed in with our search for somewhere to live. But it goes over big with the crowd.

I notice that Chris is gripping Willow's arm, his fingers digging into her flesh. She is patting his hand comfortingly.

There's a sudden commotion at the end of the street by the town gate. Great, I think, a distraction. I step up on to the base of the horse-trough to get a view. Four men are carrying a green-clad figure on a hurdle, followed by a woman wailing hysterically and being encouraged by a posse of supporters. I'd forgotten about the Ranger.

Some of our audience rush off to the new attraction, while others urge Fiona to accompany them. Cries of "Industrials!" echo down the street. The two groups coalesce.

"What's happening?" Chris asks, bemused.

"Looks like a Ranger has had an accident," I say.

"The Industrials have killed him!" a woman shrieks.

"Lady," a voice demands, "can you do aught?"

The hysterical woman is quickly told of Fiona's miraculous powers.

Fiona approaches the injured man and smooths the hair away from his face. Her lips move, but in spite of the open-mouthed silence of the crowd, I can't hear anything. She runs her hands down the man's body and the men carrying the hurdle stiffen at the extra weight. Idly I wonder what she thinks she's doing, if "thinks" is the right word in her case.

Suddenly the man takes a long, shuddering breath. His eyes open, shrink in fear, then fix on Fiona and relax.

"Ask Master Fern for a poultice to put on his wound," Fiona tells the woman.

I can't help thinking that we'll be welcome to stay if Fiona's good for business.

The stretcher moves on and I'm left wondering how we can get Fiona out of this crowd and up to Fern's attic where we can tie her up. But I don't have long to worry about that, because just then two new Rangers appear.

"You're to come with us," one of them tells Fiona with the sort of leer that turds with power develop.

"Her's done nothing wrong," Willow protests loudly, involving the crowd.

"If you know what's good for you, you'll keep

your nose out of other people's business," the Ranger tells her.

The crowd seems to stiffen. I feel it and so does the other Ranger.

"The Warden wants to welcome her to Werham. That's all," he tells Willow, so that the crowd can hear.

"Do not worry," Fiona says serenely. "Everything is planned."

From where I stand, everything's anything but planned. In fact, things are running out of control. With Doug and her going their own ways I'm beginning to get an idea of what it feels like to be dumped.

Fiona's words persuade the crowd to let her pass, but I notice that it presses on the Rangers and they have to shoulder their way through.

Neither Chris nor I volunteer to accompany her. She's on her own from now on.

# *UNWANTED GUESTS*

I am stuck in an outhouse attached to the scullery waiting for Willow to find an opportune moment to give her dad the glad news that I'm back and Fiona is under arrest. According to Willow, that was what the Warden's invitation amounted to. Innocent little me hadn't realized. I thought he was just into miracles like the rest of the unwashed citizenry.

I am sitting on a pile of logs thinking that there must, therefore, be woodcutters, and how appropriate that is in this nightmare fairy tale. I expect there are witches as well, and that Fiona will end up being burnt at the stake. Chris can pray for her.

The more I think about the other three, the odder things seem. Statistically I should have woken up with a fairer cross-section of my peers than these freaks. What kind of people were the clever old Vice Chancellor's tests designed to select? Cancel that line of thought, or where does it leave me?

A garden of bonsai stalactites hangs above my head. Drying herbs for Master Fern's decoctions. In the gloom I see a light bulb hanging in a seine net of spiders' webs. Plaited onions hang like wizened skulls. It *is* possible to survive without freezers, though why anyone would want to, I can't imagine.

I shift on my pile of logs and swear. I try to calculate. Impossible. But the answer is fifty years and four weeks.

There comes a sudden clang of metal through the wall and a furious cranking of the water pump. The door to my hidy-hole opens into the garden, so I poke my head out to hear what's going on in the scullery.

Distantly, Master Fern's voice buzzes.

Willow's voice comes through the scullery window. "If you were so hungry you could have fetched yourself some bread and cheese."

Another whine from Master Fern.

"Well, in that case," Willow tells him, "you can fill your belly with your precious dignity until I come home."

Willow has potential. Not the doormat I first thought. She comes out of the kitchen door and winks at me. "I'll tell him you're staying when his belly's full."

"Something else," I say. "I'm starting my period. What do I use?"

"Wait in the dry store and I'll bring you the necessaries."

Willow is back in a few seconds. "Here. I keep them in the cupboard by the range. Nice 'n' cosy."

She gives me a bundle of rags. There's a piece long enough for a belt, and a frayed strip which is torn at each end into two long ribbons.

Willow looks at me quizzically. "Where've you spent your life? You puts..."

"I get the idea," I say.

She giggles at my expression. "I must go and see to his lordship."

I struggle under the heavy skirt to fix the rags and remember once hearing a boy tell his mate that he didn't get anywhere with a girl the previous night because she had her rags up. I see now where the expression comes from. Must have survived a century of tampons.

I pull myself straight and do not feel confident. I am not going to live here. That is non-negotiable. Time is the difference. In this peasant society it's seasons, moons, menses that rule. I want a civilization that runs on nanoseconds.

Willow returns.

"What's going to happen to Fiona?" I ask.

She shrugs. "She's a stranger and she's healed people. Warden will want to see that there's no pollution in her."

"What if he decides there is?"

"She could be whipped till she repents or put in the stocks."

"Can she have a solicitor?"

"What's that?"

Bloody, bloody, bloody, I think. Fiona will say something to sink us. She and Ralf drew attention to themselves. So long as we merge in no one bothers about us – as far as we know. This is not an efficient police state, just a vicious peasant society. How long till Fiona leads the Rangers on a floral dance to the Base? Can Chris and I rescue her? Will Willow help?

"Come on," she says. "No use worrying. Dad's too busy eating to bother about what's going on in the kitchen. You could do with a bite, I dare say."

We go into the kitchen and Willow looks to see if Master Fern is still eating. She beckons me into the passage. I look through a crack by the hinges of the door to the living-room. Master Fern and Chris are sitting at opposite ends of the table eating stolidly. Neither shows any pleasure. Willow clamps her hand over her mouth and rolls her eyes.

There's a sudden sharp knock on the door at the end of the passage. We both jump and look at each other, paralyzed for a moment. There's the scrape of a chair from the living-room.

Willow comes alive again. "I'll get it, Father," she calls.

She signals to me to hide under the stairs behind a loose curtain. There's just room to stand between stacks of wooden trays containing dried leaves of various kinds.

Willow opens the door. Round the curtain I see the tall figure of a man step into the hall without being invited. He's dressed in the habit of a monk.

Willow curtsies quickly.

"Take me to Master Fern, girl," the figure orders.

In the dim light of the passage I can't make out the monk's features clearly, but he appears to be old and austere. Willow leads him through to the living-room.

I hear Master Fern say, "Brother Soil! This is an honour." But he sounds as though the honour is as welcome as dying for one's country.

Brother Soil? The name rings bells which don't get an immediate response.

"Master Fern," Brother Soil says, like a Mafioso greeting a relative who's for the chop.

I come out from under the stairs and put my eye to the living-room door again. Willow's listening from the kitchen doorway.

"I hear you have guests," Brother Soil says.

"Only my kinsman from Sarum," Master Fern replies quickly. "The other three he met on his journey. I gave them a night's lodging as befits the demands of hospitality. They've departed. I know not where." He gabbles, explaining too much.

Brother Soil turns to Chris. "So you're Master Fern's kin from Sarum?"

Brother! The video message comes back to me. Is this ancient monk Matthew? My brother? Old enough to be my grandfather!

No, he isn't, wasn't and is not going to be. End. Finis.

"Apprentice Salt, at your service, sir." Chris

gives a little bow.

"Have you lost your savour, Apprentice Salt?" Brother Soil asks softly.

"If I had, I should be fit only to be trampled underfoot."

"You know your gospel, Apprentice Salt. An unusual accomplishment in one of your age."

"It seems we both remember Matthew."

All right, I admit it. Chris is good (in a limited way). I don't know what they're referring to, but he's got in a mention of Matthew.

"I've never seen my kin in Sarum," Master Fern begins to say.

Brother Soil turns on him. "Master Fern, I did not come here to discuss your family. Go and mix me a phial of the prescription you reserve for me. And, Master Fern," he pauses, "make it strong."

Master Fern swallows. "The acute astringent?"

"What else?"

"I don't know whether I have ... I don't like supplying..."

"Master Fern, one who has procured a miscarriage for the Warden's wife, without her husband's knowledge either of it or the father, is in no position to develop scruples."

"I never ... how did you...?"

"It is a dangerous game you play, Master Fern. Those with power have been known to turn on their dogs." Brother Soil lays a hand on Master Fern's shoulder. The herbalist trembles. "Now fetch me the prescription."

Master Fern stumbles towards the door. I do not bother to hide. Fear will keep him silent.

When he sees me, surprise then rage bring his reptilian features to life. Because a girl has witnessed his humiliation he feels it more. He scuttles along the passage into his shop.

I return to the crack in the door. Brother Soil is facing me for the first time. His face is gaunt, pockmarked. I try to peel off the lines of age to see if he really is Matthew, but I don't know whether I'm discovering resemblances or imposing them. Fifty years: he's nothing to do with me.

"You have a ready wit, Apprentice Salt," Brother Soil says quickly, "but you cannot live by wit alone."

"From what you said to Master Fern, that is how you seem to live."

"Many people owe me their lives and free their consciences from debt by repaying me with information." He stares at Chris. "For instance, a little bird who lives in the greenwood told me that your company once numbered five."

"Only four of us journeyed to Werham."

"The one I was thinking of met with an accident in the fields."

Ralf, I think. How much does he know?

"I know of no accident," Chris claims.

"It is as well that you do not. He was a carrier of that pollution which brought judgement upon the world. You were fortunate that my little bird found the photograph he carried. It was that which brought me here." Brother Soil pauses for a second. "But what concerns me now is the one in the Warden's custody, the Lady Fiona, as the mob calls her. Is she likely to mention the carrier of pollution? You can see the misunderstanding which would arise if she did." He smiles grimly.

"The Lady Fiona is unwell. Her words cannot be relied upon as evidence."

"It is a long time since I have heard such an idea expressed, and the Warden will not think thus." Brother Soil stares into the distance. "I hear also that some Industrials have escaped or been released. Coincidence on coincidence. Now, the Warden of Werham is a lazy fool who seeks the most comfortable route to the grave, but there are others who will order events into a pattern dangerous to you."

"What would you advise, Brother Soil?"

"Serve your apprenticeship with Master Fern but be prepared to leave quickly." He gropes in the folds of his habit and draws out a money-bag. "This will support you and pay for your indenture. Bargain with Master Fern. He is venal, but I doubt that he is your match."

"I thank you for your charity," Chris says, not deviating from his role. "It is hard to make one's way in the world as an orphan."

"That leaves the Lady Fiona," Brother Soil murmurs. "Do you agree that it would be better if she did not speak?"

"It would seem to be dangerous if she did."

"The prescription Master Fern prepares will stop her tongue. A few drops in her food or drink is all that is required."

"You don't mean to kill her?" Chris demands sharply.

"The potion is a relaxant, but a side-effect is that it paralyses the vocal cords. No one will be able to squeeze a word from her."

"Torture?" Chris whispers.

"Anything is permissible to prevent pollution. Your ignorance alarms me, Apprentice Salt. Guard your tongue until your education is complete." Brother Soil snaps suddenly back into the tone he used on arrival.

Master Fern emerges from the shop and elbows me aside. Chris shoves the money-bag inside his jerkin.

Brother Soil rears cadaverously over the herbalist. "You have a promising apprentice here, Master Fern. Teach him well. All your arts. *All.* I shall follow his progress with interest." He takes the phial from Master Fern and conceals it in the folds of his habit. "I go to see the Warden. I shall commend your skill to him – and to his good lady wife."

Master Fern bows his thanks.

I dart back under the stairs and Master Fern scurries to let Brother Soil out. When he's gone Master Fern goes into his shop and slams the door.

I go in to Chris.

"Did you see who was here?"

"I was watching."

"Was he your brother?"

I shrug. "No idea. But he seems willing to help."

"He said he'd seen the photo Ralf took. That means he knows you're alive." Chris seems quite excited. "That's why he's helping us."

"If he remembers what I look like after fifty years."

"But Fiona," Chris groans. "What have I agreed to?"

"It's necessary," I tell him. "Besides, your agreement wasn't important. Brother Soil had decided what he was going to do before he came here."

"But to strike her dumb," Chris repeats with a zombie-like expression.

"Fiona's already in a world of her own," I say. "He has no choice. He's not survived fifty years by being squeamish."

Perhaps he is my brother after all.

# *THE HIGH WARDEN'S HARVEST*

I'm lying on my mattress and debating whether it wouldn't be safer to get out of this dump and back to the Base rather than waiting for the rural Gestapo to come for me. I've got my escape route planned. I'll be out of the attic window, down the thatch, on to the scullery roof and down the apple tree before the Rangers are up two flights of stairs, and I'll be paddling along the stream before they've got past Willow's outrage at the invasion of her maidenly privacy.

I wonder whether Brother Soil has persuaded the Warden to let him see Fiona and given her the gob-stopper drops yet.

Brother, brother, brother? Having had a good look at him, I can say with total certainty that I do not want that antique fanatic for a relative. But the possibility still nags. Suppose *I'd* lived through the last fifty years and *he'd* jumped. How would I feel at sixty-five with him still eighteen?

I'd throttle the little bastard.

Willow is in bed snoring. "Are you awake?" I ask superfluously. It has belatedly occurred to me that even though Fiona may not be able to speak she could be forced to write, if anyone thinks of it. Has that possibility occurred to Brother Soil? Perhaps he could break her fingers while she can't scream.

The sound of Willow getting up wakes me. Early morning light filters through the rags and broken panes. Pastel colours. Très garrety. Only needs an easel.

"Willow, can you write?"

"Why should a body bother teaching I a thing like that?" she answers without appearing surprised at this morning greeting. "There's enough to know in running a house."

I push back the covers and get a whiff of myself. Turbot. "Phew! Willow, I don't know how to look after myself in this world. You'd better teach me."

"What d'you want to know?"

"Keeping clean for a start."

Willow giggles and tosses me a hairbrush. "A hundred strokes each way, morning and night. I warm a basin of water for the rest of me before Father's up, and have a top and tail in the kitchen. I put dried petals in the water so I do smell sweet. You never know when Mr Right might come along, do 'ee?"

"Is that all you think about?"

"What else is there?"

I laugh. But her idea of a relationship is control from a subservient position. Not mine.

We creep downstairs so as not to disturb Master Fern.

After Willow has blown life into the fire in the range, we wash; me copying her.

"Do you always get up before your father?" I ask, knowing the answer.

"Of course." Willow giggles at the idea that anything else is possible. "His lordship would be mightily put out if his shaving water weren't hot and his breakfast ready."

"How do you wake up? Don't you ever oversleep?"

"I've got a blackbird gives I a call. Mind you, after midsummer revels I were so all-over content I were a bit late the next morning." She gives me a knowing wink.

We eat thick rashers of bacon and bread sopping with fat. Just what I crave. Stuff the penance of health foods.

"Willow," I say with my mouth full, "I need to go out of town to collect something. About that size." I indicate half a slice of bread which is about as big as the radio.

"I don't suppose you'll be wanting no one looking at it neither," Willow says innocently.

"Be better if no one saw it," I admit. "I don't like to upset people."

"Well now. If you were to go collecting herbs and were to put a cloth in the bottom of a basket which I were to give 'ee, that would be a very useful morning's work, I'd say. You might keep an eye open for early blackberries an' all."

"Willow, you're as devious as I am," I compliment her. "Don't you want to know about us?"

"Oh, I'm as curious as the next. But I reckon I'm a fair judge of people and I don't believe Chris or Doug are the sort as'll do anything malicious. In any case, I doubt I'd understand what they're about."

I note she doesn't include me.

Then she adds, "You think more like a man than a maid."

"A girl can think as well as any boy," I object. "We're equal to men."

"That's as maybe. But it's best not to let on. Especially to my dad." She laughs. Manipulator.

The advances women made in the century before I took the sleep have been swept away with technology. Willow does not even know what I mean by equality.

"You see," Willow says, looking at my expression, "you're thinking I don't even understand what you mean. Well, that's as may be, but that don't worry me – though it would you."

"You don't miss much, do you?"

When Master Fern and Apprentice Salt have been served their breakfasts, Willow gives Pansy, who's arrived late, a telling-off and instructions about her morning chores. Then Willow and I go out, large baskets riding on our hips, like extras in *Draculaville*.

"I'll walk with you to the gate, then do my shopping, such as it is, on the way back."

But our plans change when we reach the crossroads. There's a large crowd gathered round the stocks.

Fiona, is my first thought.

"Use your basket to push a way through," Willow says, and does so expertly.

"It's the Watch," she tells me when she can see. "The Rangers be a-putting him in the stocks."

Two of the local storm troopers are manhandling a gawping, bleary-eyed fellow.

I'm surprised to find that the first thing the spectators do when the Rangers finish is to pelt him not with vegetables but with questions. In videoland medieval peasants are never without baskets of unwanted (and at the time undiscovered) tomatoes.

It seems that at least part of his story is known.

"How many o' they Industrials were there, Mr Watch?" a voice wants to know.

"Six huge fellas," the Watch asserts.

"Sure you weren't a-seeing double?" someone calls out, earning a chorus of jeers in support.

"'Tis true, I swears it. I fought like a ... like a—"

"Bag o' wind," someone suggests.

"—a wild boar. But there were too many. Girt, murderous barbarians..."

"Where's Weed?" a woman demands.

"They did take 'ee. To eat," he adds. "So they tole I."

"Oh, yars," a scornful voice puts in. "An' I

suppose they took your peg o' cider to wash 'ee down."

"I don't know no more. I were knocked cold."

"If you were so brave, why's Warden put you in stocks?"

"What's happened?" I ask Willow.

"The Industrials who escaped stole some horses in the night and took the Watch's boy with 'en."

I am trying to jigsaw pieces of information together. It has to be Doug and his Industrials. The more I know what he's capable of the more I see him as a boil on the bum. And I still don't know what makes him tick.

I become aware of a hand plucking at my sleeve. The crowd has grown denser. For a second I don't recognize the face on a lower level to mine. Then I exclaim, "Cluck!" The village idiot.

"The – the Lady Fiona," he says. "W-Warden has sent her to Sarum."

I clutch Willow's arm. "Have I understood him right?"

Cluck repeats what he's said, stammering more the second time.

Willow lets out a cry which cuts through the crowd's banter with the Watch.

"What's Warden done with the Lady Fiona?"

"She be s-sent to S-Sarum," Cluck repeats, nodding rapidly.

"A Ranger did come from High Warden," someone adds.

"Aye, an' I saw the Warden's carriage leave not

half an hour since with the blinds down, an' the Ranger were a-riding behind," another voice tells us.

From the crowd arises a growl. It starts in no one spot, as far as I can tell, but swells up around me, and makes the hair on the nape of my neck rise. I feel the crowd move in unison and I get this urge to go with it. But at the same time it makes me feel slimy.

I dig my nails into my palms. "I'm my own mistress," I assert, teeth clenched.

"To the Warden's house!" someone cries, and the organism slides away.

The Rangers, who have been standing idly by listening until this point, have somehow managed to disappear. I find myself left at the crossroads with only the forgotten Watch for company.

I help myself to a cabbage from an abandoned stall and chuck it at his head.

"Anyone round here sell tomatoes?" I ask him, then make tracks for the gate. I don't have any new ideas except to let Doug know what's happened to Fiona and give him a sample of my unexpurgated vocabulary.

It turns out that my precautions for collecting the radio aren't necessary. The road and fields are deserted. It seems the excitement has been seized on as an excuse for a morning off. I put the radio in the basket and on top I strew leaves which I hope are herbs.

At seven that evening I begin to call Doug. Half

an hour later I give up. I wonder whether he's being bloody-minded or has landed himself in a mess. I hide the radio under a loose floorboard in Willow's room as instructed. Stuff Doug. I'll make my own plans.

I find Chris in the garden watching Willow work. It seems that lifting potatoes requires her to lean forward frequently with the top of her blouse unlaced.

"No luck," I tell Chris.

"It's probably deliberate."

"Why's that?" I try to sound puzzled.

Chris shrugs. "Doug doesn't want anything to do with us." He sounds petulant.

He gets on my nerves. Doug's much easier to get along with. Selfish bastards always are. Indignation and self-pity are what I can't stand – i.e. Chris.

"I'll try again at the next contact time," I say without inflexion.

Willow straightens up and looks at us. "Your friend'll be all right, I reckon."

"Why's that?" Chris asks aggressively.

Willow glances down and innocently draws a circle in the earth with her foot. "Just a feeling." She puts on an expression which overdoes the suggestion that she's remembering some incident. Chris's face goes blank. Poor sod doesn't stand a chance. She'll blow bubbles with him. "Catch." She tosses a muddy potato at him. "He's the sort people do things for. There's no use grieving about that. He'll come to no harm."

Chris seems satisfied with that.

Just then Master Fern comes to the kitchen door with the look of one who has a prepared speech to deliver. "Apprentice Salt," he begins, "I'd be greatly obliged if you would favour me with a little of your attention. If you wish to be a gardener rather than a herbalist, that can be arranged. In the meantime I have a task for you, and I should like to be able to give a good report to Brother Soil when he returns from Sarum." Having snapped out his speech he turns and stamps indoors.

I look at Chris, then at Willow. "Why would Brother Soil go to Sarum?"

"I dare say he goes to see the High Warden," Willow suggests. "They do say he's a powerful man."

"Keeping an eye on Fiona?" I wonder.

"He didn't go with her," Willow tells us. "I saw him leave when you were out collecting herbs."

"I'd better go in," Chris says, and shoots the potato back at Willow underarm so that she has to catch it low on her stomach.

"It's three days' hard walking to Sarum," Willow says, sharp as ever, "and a maid can't go alone."

"Why did the Warden send Fiona to Sarum?"

"He told the crowd that the High Warden had commanded him to send any strange persons to him without delay."

"Why should the High Warden say that?" I wonder.

Willow rolls her eyes. "Well the las' time I spoke to 'ee…"

"All right," I agree. "Stupid question."

"You can go to Sarum in four weeks."

"How's that?"

"Harvest Festival."

"I don't believe this."

"'Tis simple. Every town sends harvest pilgrims to the festival with tithes for the High Warden."

"Will Fiona be all right for four weeks?"

"That I don't know. But there's not much you can do about it an' that's a fact."

I believe her. Unless I can contact Doug and he can do something – wherever he is, if he's still alive – Fiona's on her own. But Sarum is where it's all happening, so that's where I want to be.

"All right. Give me a fork. If I'm going to be a harvest pilgrim, I'd better help get the harvest in."

I'm going native. Best camouflage, I judge.

While I dig I decide to get myself some more protection. That will be tomorrow's task.

"How do I get to have a word with the Warden's wife?" I ask Willow the next morning.

She gives me an old-fashioned look. "Without bothering the Warden, would that be?"

"Just women's talk, you might say."

"Go round to the kitchen door of the Warden's house. He won't concern himself with comings and goings there."

I do as Willow suggests.

"I've come to see the Warden's wife," I tell a cross-eyed kitchen skivvy, "about a long-lost relative."

Nice touch that, and it gets me in.

"Well, girl. Who are you?" a dim, overweight woman trying to play the grande dame splutters at me when I finally stand before her.

She is wearing a grimy red dress of some heavy material and a linen bonnet. She reminds me of the Queen of Hearts in a play version of *Alice in Wonderland* that I saw when I was about four. The old frump gave me nightmares then. Now revenge time has arrived.

"I'm a busy woman. I've no time for sluts trying to wheedle a free meal out of me with hard-luck stories."

"It's like this, Mrs Warden," I tell her, picking up a pre-Judgement china knick-knack from an ostentatious display. I toy with it while I put her in the picture vis-à-vis her position.

"Put that down," she screeches. "Do you know how much it's worth?"

I weigh it in my palm and tell her, "I supply information to interested parties about lost relatives. Particularly tiny ones lost courtesy of Master Fern."

I juggle to give her time to take that in.

She suddenly looks dog-eared. As much backbone as a boiled cabbage. Doesn't even try to bluff it out.

"What do you want?" she squeaks, throttled by a vision of her standard of living dropping to a level where she might have to work.

Having frightened the stuffing out of the old sow, I send in the friendly interrogator. No one has to suffer, so here's how to do a deal with the DA.

"I want nothing for myself," I protest. "I'm only concerned for you in your lovely house. I'm staying with Master Fern for a few weeks and everything will go on as before – providing that the Warden does not take it into his head to send me to Sarum like the Lady Fiona. If he tried that I wouldn't be able to prevent myself from saying anything I thought might interest him. If you see what I mean."

Oh, she does.

I leave with her assurance that her husband, who is putty between her ample thighs, will do exactly as she tells him. Which is precisely nothing. End of Red Queen.

Next I go to have a chat with Master Fern and ask him what the Warden would do to someone who treated his wife without his knowledge. Don't worry, I tell him, laughing, like it's a hypothetical joke. No one will say a dicky-bird so long as he doesn't get any bright ideas – like evicting me.

Then, feeling more secure, I make myself at home while I wait for Harvest Festival. But every time I venture out I get the feeling that I'm being watched. Am I paranoid, or what?

# *HARVEST PILGRIMS*

Three weeks later and I'm just like one of the family. Pansy, after being late for work several days in a row – from morning sickness, it turns out – has been given the old hurry-up pills by compassionate Master Fern. Who's the father? I wonder. I've noticed his eyes clawing at her.

I get to take over her chores while she's away, including emptying Fern's chamber pot of a morning. I now know all I want to know about surviving in this rural midden.

I'm sitting in the garden under a pear tree and instead of getting on with hoeing the sprouts, I'm musing on the possibility of the store tunnel in the Base containing weed-killer, when a small, wiry boy appears in front of me.

He's dressed in the usual Earther outfit, but there's a streetwise arrogance about him which I've not seen for fifty years.

"Cindy?" he asks.

This wakes me up. Everyone knows me as Cinnamon.

"Who wants to know?"

"I'm Vanguard," he says proudly. "I used to be Weed."

Click. The boy who disappeared when Doug and the Industrials stole the horses. Weed was supposed to be a snack, according to the Watch.

"Oh, yes," I say, "and what are you vanguard of?"

"The new times which are a-coming."

"Sounds hopeful," I encourage him. "Do you have a message for me?"

"The Steam-master says—"

"The who?"

"The Steam-master is known to you as Doug."

"Now that's clear," I say, my mind travelling faster than a sub-atomic particle, "what's the message?"

Vanguard recites: "The Steam-master is forging the instruments for a second Industrial Revolution. This society is rotten and ready to fall. Come to Sarum if you want to see some fun."

"Is Doug – the Steam-master – near Sarum?"

Vanguard nods.

That explains why there's been no radio contact: too far without a satellite link.

"What are you going to do?"

"I must return. We have work to do," Vanguard says proudly.

Sometimes things come together in a way which

makes the lame-brained think that events are directed by fate or the stars. So here I am, waiting to go to Sarum, and I get an invitation to go there. Now I *really* want to, never mind Fiona. If Doug has some scheme to get the twenty-first century back on the rails, I'm going to be there, and Vanguard's progress from a drunken watchman's assistant to Steam-master's acolyte suggests that Doug has what it takes to make things happen.

I instruct Vanguard to tell Doug where Fiona is and a week later I'm sitting in Master Fern's cart bouncing springlessly towards Sarum. Chris and Willow sit on the only seat, with the horse's arse for scenery. I am crammed in the back with the luggage. The radio is in a concealed compartment under the boards of the cart bottom.

I amuse myself by watching Chris. To see the lengths he goes to in order to avoid contact with Willow, you'd think she was a virus-carrier. She pretends to be unaware of the various parts of her anatomy which brush against him as the cart bangs over the cobbles.

What's he afraid of? Not being able to perform? Too easy. It's more like he's afraid of his desires themselves; which I take to be normal or he wouldn't have to worry about giving into them. QED, hey, McKay?

There's a huge tithing wagon ahead of us stacked with grain, potatoes, carrots, onions and root crops that I don't recognize. Swedes? Turnips? Mangle-wurzels – or are they a joke?

Peasant fodder, anyway. This is boredom on wheels. My bum's numb and so's my brain. Nothing but trees to look at. Give me posters, neon and a three-litre engine to sweep them up.

"There's a spring tithing as well," Willow tells me, balancing a tit on Chris in order to turn round. "Then yearlings and such be taken to the High Warden."

"What does he do in return for these tithes?" I ask.

Willow makes a great show of thinking. "I reckon he feeds hisself and his men," she says finally. "Oh, and he makes sure the land don't get polluted and protects us from the Industrials."

"Is the High Warden well-liked?" Chris asks.

"Not by me he 'ent," Willow laughs. "I had to give a dozen flagons of my best ale."

"Why?" Chris wants to know, indignant on her behalf.

"Well, who'd want any of Dad's old herbs for tithes?" She laughs at his obtuseness and he flushes.

We reach Blandford Forum in the early evening and meet similar tithing parties from Wey Mouth, Durnovaria, Brid and Lyme.

Willow is excited by the crowds and the size of the town. As soon as we find a secure place to park the cart, she takes Chris by the hand and drags him away. "Let's go and look at everything. Some of these big towns do send two sides of morris men. They'll be a-dancing outside the taverns to earn theyselves ale."

She leads Chris not-so-reluctantly away, and I relish the thought that he's going to disapprove of these peasant revels.

The cart's standing in what used to be a garage. Roofless now. On either side the houses have been abandoned. Our horse is grazing in an overgrown back garden. I undo a concealed catch in the bottom of the cart and pull out the radio.

It's the right time for making contact and we might be close enough now to get through, if Doug's still listening.

"Hallo? Do you hear me?" I begin, and for some reason feel foolish talking to a lump of plastic in these surroundings.

"Hallo, hallo," a voice booms. "Wait!"

The sound echoes in the ruined shell of walls. I stab wildly at the volume control, missing it twice.

The voice – not Doug's – says "Wait" again.

There's a long pause, then unmistakably Doug's voice says, "What's taken you so long?"

"Someone else chose my team for me. Over."

Doug's bark of a laugh comes back at me.

"Who was that answered my call?" I ask.

"One of my people. There's not long to go now. Everything's on the brink of collapse. Over."

"What are you planning?" I ask.

"Take out the local militia and there'll be no organized resistance. Can't say more for security reasons. It's possible that someone listens. You'll see soon enough."

"Do you know what's happened to Fiona? Over."

"She's being held in the High Warden's palace. Be careful when you enter Sarum. The Rangers have been told to look out for anyone physically more healthy than normal. Teeth in particular. They know that something's going on. I'm surprised they haven't picked you up. How much they're guessing and how much Fiona's said, I don't know. Over."

The callous bastard doesn't sound very bothered about Fiona. Perhaps he can just shut off worries he can't do anything about. I tell him about Brother Soil and Fiona.

"I'm surprised they haven't picked you up," he says again.

"Thanks. I took out some extra insurance to discourage anyone from getting too curious," I tell him.

"I thought Chris'd be OK with you," he laughs. Then, "I must go," he says suddenly. "A Ranger patrol is nearby, getting inquisitive. They amuse themselves by raiding Industrial camps and doing a bit of rape and pillage. They'll be in for a surprise if they try that here. Out."

And that's it.

I fetch some bread, cheese and ale from the cart and sit against what remains of the back wall of the garage.

I liked Doug's "One of my people". How many's he got? He's as cagey as ever with information where his plans are concerned. But I could feel the drive in him even over the radio. Does he plan to bring back the twenty-first century? Steam-master? I remember again the paddle-steamer he made.

The horse comes and nuzzles my neck. "Get lost," I tell it. "You're history."

I switch on the radio again and press *search*. The figures dissolve in a blur. It runs through the sequence then begins again. There's no human transmission on any frequency. All channels are dead. What's the use of being alive after the end of the world?

# *HARVEST FESTIVAL*

The next morning we set off so early the birds would have legitimate grounds for complaint at being disturbed. The wagon train has lengthened with carts from other towns, and some of the peasantry who have alcohol poisoning have to be loaded on like sacks.

Chris sits up front with Willow again and stares censoriously at the horse's arse. Perhaps he's identifying with it. Willow winks at me. I wonder for the umpteenth time what she sees in such a juiceless specimen.

After a few minutes' motion yesterday's bruises feel as if they're being puréed. I focus on the unspoiled countryside and yearn for some industrial pollution and ancillary products. Then I get to thinking about the Base and the cool capsules of the sleepers and I wish I was back there. What's the point of letting them wake up to this? I could go back, reset the dates so that they'd go on hibernating, and live there in a one-girl luxury universe. If I got lonely I could wake one up for company. But after the experience I've had with my present team, I'd have to be desperate. What would suit me would be an android I could programme. Total control over another person.

The cart hits a rock and a stab of pain ignites my natural resentment and ends my depression-induced reverie.

It's evening when we get to Sarum. The spire of the Cathedral is the biggest human structure I've seen so far. And that's not new by about a thousand years.

"Be a sly little maid," Willow tells me as we approach the city gates.

"No problem," I say. After a month I can talk like her – and that sums up my two choices: stay here and sink or go back to the Base. Unless Doug's got a third lined up for me.

We cross a causeway over an undrained marsh to a gate in the city wall. This place is not like Werham. The wall is high and in good repair.

There are Rangers examining every cart as it enters the city. If they are, as Doug said, searching for people like us, then they've forgotten by the time we arrive. They're alternately brusque and over-familiar. The aim appears to be to instil the same servility in visitors that the good citizens of Sarum display. They rummage in each cart like sniffer dogs, trying to provoke a reaction so that they can crush it. Their search is careless and the radio remains undiscovered.

I find that my biggest worry is Chris giving us away. I can feel his indignation consuming him. But the Rangers are more interested in Willow and me. A pig-faced Ranger shoulders him aside so that he can get to us. He fondles Willow while getting her to unpack a bundle. The other suggests how he could entertain me after we've parked the cart and gropes me in case I'm a bit slow to take his meaning, me being only a simple country girl.

I give an exaggerated smile and fart in his palm.

"Industrial bitch," he says and slaps the horse.

The cart jumps forward and Willow grabs Chris and pushes him through the gate.

"Why do you put up with it?" Chris demands, as though it's all Willow's fault.

She shrugs. "That's just the way things be. Don't you worry about it, my duck."

Chris falls silent and walks stiffly alongside the horse. Suddenly I can read his thoughts. Under the rigid exterior he's directing a stream of obscene abuse at Willow and praying for forgiveness at the same time. I'd bet his cherry on it.

We follow another cart to a field where all the pilgrims are camping. The tithing wagon is taken off to be unloaded into the High Warden's storehouses inside the Cathedral Close, which is a walled area within the city. I'm surprised that, in contrast to the walls, the ordinary houses are in a worse state than those in Werham. But when I get a glimpse of the houses in the Close they appear in good condition. They're Georgian, or something of the sort, with windows divided into small squarish panes and, what's really surprising, they've all got glass in them. It looks like a case of ruling elite and downtrodden peasantry.

That night we sleep in a makeshift tent attached to the side of the cart. We're packed rather tight and I note that in her sleep Willow's arm inadvertently falls across Chris. He doesn't appear to notice. Now what makes me think that neither of them is as deeply asleep as they seem?

I toss and turn for a while. It's too risky to call Doug and eventually I fall asleep wondering what the ruthless bastard's got planned.

In the morning Willow begins to harness the horse.

"Why're you doing that?" I ask.

"To go to the Harvest Festival, of course."

"Isn't it in the Cathedral?"

"Why no!" she exclaims. "That's soft of me. I thought you knew. It's at the henge."

"Oh," I say, none the wiser. "Is it far?"

"Half a day's journey. We'll camp there tonight."

Another creaking procession and four hours later there's chaos as we reach a vast gypsy-like campsite. I take the horse's head and try to find a convenient place to stake a claim without being trampled under-hoof. We tie up eventually by a couple of spindly trees which will guide us back when the Harvest Festival is over. It's like an old-style music festival plus horse dung.

It isn't until I clamber up on the cart to unload the tent that I can see beyond a rise in the ground and recognize where we are. It's obvious once I know.

"We're at Stone-bloody-henge!" I exclaim.

Only it's no longer a ruin. The outer sarsen stones make an unbroken circle of arches and in the centre the five trilithons tower over a flat altar stone.

"Bring on the Druids," I laugh.

"I feared as much," Chris says, grimly unimpressed. "They've reverted to a pagan nature religion."

"Come on," Willow says. "We want a good place to see the sport."

She leads the way towards the stones, using her elbows and her picnic basket to shift people out of the way. I get the feeling she's so excited by what's going to happen that she's on a high.

We come to a circle of corn sheaves lying on their sides. They're on a mound along the edge of a ditch which is some way back from the stones. I can see four priests wearing green chasubles inside the arches, making preparations. Rangers patrol the area between the stones and the ditch like bouncers at a concert.

Then the warm-up act comes on. It's a side of morris men with their latest number, one that involves hopping up and down and clashing staves. Their faces are blacked and they're dressed in layers of green ribbons which flap like leaves. There's a fool with a red face. He has an inflated pig's bladder on a stick and is free to improvise. Whenever anyone's temporarily blinded by upending a flagon he darts forward and cuffs the offender with his bladder, which makes him spill his ale down his neck. This goes over big with the punters. Willow hoots and tries to persuade Chris to take a drink, which he does – but only when the bladder's nowhere near.

The fool's other joke is to thrust his stick forward through his legs and make obscene gestures. This joke is a favourite with those women who look as though their only hope of pulling a bloke would be coming across a blindfolded gorilla. When that side of morris men has finished another replaces it. No expense spared.

In the distance I see a thin column of smoke in the still air.

"What's that?" I ask Willow.

I get a reply from the peasant on the sheaf next to mine. "That's Industrial smoke, missy. They're busy at their forges. Have been this past month." I shudder on cue. He gives me a gap-toothed leer. "Don't worry thyself. I'll look after 'ee."

"Well, that's right kind of 'ee," I say. "I'll just have to see that my betrothed's agreeable. He's that fine big Ranger over yonder."

The man pulls dejectedly away and goes back to his flagon.

A month of smoke, I think. About the time

Doug has been busy with his people. Willow gets out the picnic. I chew on a thick chunk of brown bread spread with red and brown dripping. It's salty. I take a drink. Most of the audience (or congregation or whatever it is) seem to be half drunk already.

Chris points. A coach, followed by a wagon, has pulled up on the far side of the central semicircle of stones. The coach is the first closed vehicle I've seen. Someone important, I guess.

"The High Warden and the Bishop be in there," Willow tells us. She is flushed in anticipation.

A box is placed below the door of the coach and a huge figure levers itself out.

"The High Warden," Willow whispers.

He is so gross he can hardly walk. Two Rangers help him down and support him to a seat near the altar stone. He is dressed in a cream chemise which ripples like silk, and over it a loose velvet robe which is red with gold piping on the seams. He is perspiring copiously.

The Bishop follows him out of the coach but no one assists him. Is that an indication of where power lies? I wonder.

The High Warden glances impatiently at the Bishop. Everyone is silent. The morris men have vanished. The Bishop takes his place by the altar stone.

"We are gathered here today to give thanks for the harvest," he begins in a high voice which is amplified by the stones.

"Let us pray.

"O Lord our God, we thank Thee for Thy bounty. Thou tendst us as a loving father tends his children and providst for our every need. Thou guidest us as a shepherd guides his flock. Thou art the great gardener and in Thy hands rests the purity of the land.

"Let us sing 'For the Blessings of This Day'."

The morris men's musicians set about the hymn with vigour. They're scattered round the circle of spectators and different sections finish each verse a bar early or late. No one seems concerned. The crowd roars its slurred praises and reminds me of a midnight carol service my mother dragged me to in a fit of sentiment, where the congregation's breath gave the church the atmosphere of a brewery.

As the hymn stutters to its end a towering figure made of straw is raised in the centre of the stones. It is balanced on the top of a pole and dominates the henge.

"It's a corn dolly," Chris exclaims.

"It's the Virgin Mary," Willow corrects him.

The peasant next to me is cheering and dribbling. His excitement at the sight of this second-rate bit of basketwork seems out of proportion. My stomach tells me that this is the intro to a vicious spectator sport.

The Bishop's voice becomes audible once more.

"The Virgin Mother offered the seed of her womb as a sacrifice, without which the land would be barren. Each autumn her virginity is restored and she becomes one with the earth so that in spring the land may bring new life to sustain us. Thus is the miracle of the Resurrection given substance."

I see that Chris's hand is clamped round Willow's wrist. "This is blasphemy," he hisses. "This is the real pollution."

"Hush now," Willow whispers. She strokes his head with her free hand. "We'll set everything to rights later."

"What can stop the Resurrection?" the Bishop demands, his voice rising.

"Pollution!" the crowd roars. I hasten to join in for the sake of verisimilitude and give the drooling peasant next to me a self-satisfied leer. No pollution here: we're true believers. Looking at him, I wonder what it's like to spend your life brain-damaged.

There's silence. The crowd is straining to detect the first ripple of movement that will herald the start of the next act. It comes from the wagon. A figure like a scarecrow with arms and legs encased in sheaves suddenly sits up then jumps off the end. Beneath the straw is the green of a Ranger uniform.

A second figure like the first stands up in the wagon and between them they drag a bundle of rags to the tailgate. It falls to the ground in an angular heap. The scarecrows drag it to its feet. I see now that it is dressed in a monk's habit.

"Don't look," Chris whispers quickly. He's ahead of me.

Brother Soil, I realize; and I watch.

The old monk is dragged stumbling to the altar stone and spread-eagled on his back. The priests, who've been scenery up to this point, leap forward and grab his arms and legs. They bear down on him so that his body arches against the stone.

The High Warden draws a scroll from the folds of his robe and hands it to the Bishop to read.

"This is the judgement of the High Warden's Court," the Bishop intones. "The man known as Brother Soil is no brother to the land, but its polluter." The crowd lets out its breath with a hiss. "He has been spreading corruption through the countryside since before the Judgement. He is an agent of death. How many of you have suffered blighted crops, barren animals, strange sicknesses after he has passed through your district?"

There's a murmur of assent and vigorous nodding from the spectators. I find that my head wants to join in.

"His evil has been uncovered by the unceasing vigilance of the High Warden, our protector, who preserves the purity of the land." The High Warden wearily raises his hand to acknowledge the crowd's plaudits. "Now let the polluter purge his corruption and fructify the soil." The Bishop lowers his scroll.

The giant corn dolly gets lowered on to Brother Soil's prone form in an embrace which strikes me as ludicrous, but seems to turn the peasants on. My neighbour somehow inserts his hand through the sheaf and up between my legs. There's a lot of swigging of ale, so I smile and offer him a swallow from our flagon. Unfortunately my hand slips and I knock out one of his teeth. He rolls into the ditch in front of us and falls asleep.

"Don't watch this," Chris repeats.

There are hoarse shouts of encouragement from the congregation.

The corn dolly rises into the air again and the scarecrows step forward. One produces what looks like a large money-bag. The other positions himself by Brother Soil's head and forces his mouth open.

The Bishop's voice resumes.

"We are all dust. From dust we were fashioned and to dust we return."

The scarecrow plunges his hand into the bag and something fine trickles between his fingers. "Earth to earth." Dry soil. But it is spilling into Brother Soil's open mouth and nostrils. "Ashes to ashes."

Whoever dreamed this up had a macabre sense of humour. Brother Soil is slowly suffocating. A cough blows back some soil, but when he tries to suck in air he inhales more dust.

"In the sure and certain hope of the Resurrection." His body arches spasmodically. "Unless we die we cannot share in the Resurrection." Brother Soil's body is soon still. "The body is the seed." He seems to have shrunk.

The corn dolly is lowered beside the altar stone

and removed from its pole. I notice for the first time an oblong hole at the foot of the altar. The corn dolly is laid in it and covered with earth.

The crowd sighs ecstatically.

Music strikes up. The High Warden is being levered into his coach. His languid posture suggests that the spectacle has been put on for the benefit of inferiors.

Spectators are grabbing each other and I get the impression that very shortly promiscuity is going to be the order of the day. I note that Willow has a firm grip on Chris. I can see that an execution could be an aphrodisiac, but this one doesn't grab me that way.

"I'm going to find my betrothed," I tell the peasant in the ditch and anyone else with any plans which might include me.

I stumble backwards off my sheaf. My last view of the scene is of Willow holding a flagon to Chris's mouth and him gulping greedily.

The crowd thins quickly as I hurry away from the henge. A drunken lout tries to grab me and I give him a good-humoured two-handed shove. He falls over backwards and cracks his head on a lump of white stone. Two pilgrims who are already horizontal find this vastly amusing.

The campsite is deserted. I find our cart and lean against it.

What have I just witnessed? Nothing. The death of a stranger in a strange land. Not my brother. I'd already decided that, hadn't I? What was I supposed to do even if he had been? Get myself killed like Dad did trying to rescue sister Suzy? They'd all sacrificed themselves to keep me alive, hadn't they? So it would have been an ungrateful waste of their lives to have got myself killed trying to save my not-brother.

That's all right then. I'm not guilty of anything. Just the same as always.

# *THE ATTACK*

I've had it with peasants. I dig out the radio and let it absorb some solar power. At seven o'clock I call Doug and get his radio operator telling me to wait. How does he do it? He's a magnet. People follow him. Want to do what he says. He doesn't have to blackmail them.

"Are you at Stonehenge?" his voice suddenly asks.

"Yes. Where are you? Over."

"Can you see smoke to the north?"

"Is that you? Look, I'm pissed off with peasants. Over."

"Can you get away unobserved?"

"I'll have to circle the henge. There's a bit of a party going on there. Over."

"Go to the east. I'll send people to meet you."

"What about Chris? He's partying with Willow. Over."

"Tell them to go to Sarum and wait there till I come. Out."

That's it. A man of few words. Not so hot on the "overs" but never misses an "out". So what did I want, an agony aunt? Some news about Fiona would have been a nice touch.

I find a stone that looks like chalk, and scratch a message on the cart for Chris. Then I go, with my commando knife tucked below my bosom ready to administer quietus to any peasant who has ideas about forcible frolics.

The party has swelled and the circle I'm forced to make to avoid heaving drunks and heaving buttocks is so large that it's past nine o'clock before I'm north of the henge. I'm marching off into a flat wilderness, it's almost dark and I'm beginning to think this wasn't such a good idea, when a group of riders rises up out of a hollow in the plateau.

"You're a long way from home, Earther." The speaker is a girl.

"Further than you know," I reply. "If you're an Industrial, you'd better keep clear of Stonehenge."

"It's her," a man says. "She's no Earther."

"Who sent you?" I ask.

"The Steam-master."

"Good. I'm Cindy," I say. "Have you got a spare horse?" No need to mention that I can't ride the thing even if they have. Just sound confident.

"You can ride behind Tappet," the girl says.

My antennae twitch. Do I sense a touch of hostility? Yes, I do. I'm rarely wrong in these matters. So why should she see me as a threat? Click – Doug! She thinks I might be competition.

"How's Douggie?" I ask. "I mean the Steam-master. You been looking after him OK?"

Tappet leans down and swings me up behind him. Then we clop off and I don't get an answer. The man's silhouette against the sky tickles a synapse.

"Were you one of the Industrials at Werham?" I ask Tappet.

"Aye," he agrees.

"Who's the girl?"

"Tricity. Darwin's daughter."

I remember: Darwin the scientist.

The horse moves at an unhurried pace, I'm relieved to say, since I'm sitting side-saddle without a saddle. I cling on to Tappet and enjoy an unwashed smokey-sweaty smell; makes a change from unwashed beery-sweaty. I hope the horses know where we're going because before long I can't see a thing. No distant flickers of car headlights. No glow in the sky from cities. Just stars, like in a planetarium. When will the lights come up?

"We're going to our factory," Tappet says when I ask.

I wonder what "factory" means to them. Probably blow Henry Ford's mind. After two or three hours I find out. We enter a valley dotted with fires. The place is guarded, but I don't notice the sentries until we're past them.

The valley is a scrap-metal yard. Bits of every metal object I ever cared about are piled in mutilated heaps next to crude forges. There are black mounds with glowing slits in them. Charcoal fires, I guess. Greater temperature than wood. Someone's been a busy boy.

There are buildings which are a cross between huts and tents made from a kaleidoscope of rubbish from my world. Outside them are cooking fires over which troglodytes are stewing unidentifiable lumps in cauldrons. We stop at a large building which reminds me of a Mongolian nomad's tent. Tappet lowers me to the ground. My legs are numb and I stagger. The girl scowls and holds aside a leather curtain to let me in.

The structure is supported by metal girders lashed together with leather thongs. A doorless fridge serves as a cupboard for pottery bowls. There are no tables. The air is heavy. Light comes from a burning wick in a dish of oil. On the far side of the room sits a figure on a pile of sheep skins like Ghengis Khan in his tent – Doug.

"Bloody hell," I say. "This is worse than Werham."

"More initiative here," Doug tells me. "There has to be to survive the culling carried out by the Rangers."

"What're you up to?"

"We're just about to conquer the world."

He smiles enigmatically. I feel like laughing, but suddenly don't think it would be wise. Did anyone laugh at Alexander the Great? He was about Doug's age, I think.

"I could use a drink," I say to give myself time

to think. I sit down on a bundle of fleeces and wonder about ticks. Do they like people's blood as well as sheep's?

Doug gestures to Tricity, who produces a pottery mug with some hot infusion in it. Herb tea, I guess.

"So where and when are you starting?" I ask Doug.

"Sarum. Tomorrow night."

"The people might not want to be part of your brave new world."

"The people will be happy enough to have a change of masters." He stares at me. "You've survived for a month as an Earther. How did you avoid being arrested?"

Does he suspect me of being a spy?

"Curtseying to the Warden and wiggling my arse at the Rangers," I say.

"Exactly. Everyone goes in fear of the Rangers and the Wardens. Take them out and like any totalitarian state it collapses." He smiles again. "That's what we're going to do in Sarum."

"Brother Soil was sacrificed at Stonehenge," I tell him.

"I knew he was going to be. It fits in with my plan."

Oh well then (I don't say), that makes it all worthwhile. I begin to suspect I've got another nutcase on my hands. One hundred per cent record. Why hasn't he mentioned Fiona? Doesn't she fit into his plans?

"Have you heard anything about Fiona?" I ask.

"Is she still alive?"

"The High Warden has her." He doesn't seem concerned. "Nothing's happened to her."

"How do you know?"

"Vanguard is not the only Earther to change sides. We're well-informed."

"She won't be killed as a hostage when you attack Sarum, will she?"

He laughs at my ignorance. "They won't have the chance."

I feign tiredness and I'm shown a place to sleep. More fleeces. I leave Doug to Tricity, who's hanging around, but I don't think she's going to get much joy there. He's the same, but changed. Focused now and indifferent to distractions. People are assessed in the light of their usefulness in fulfilling his purpose. He's learned to smile without humour. So where does that leave me? Relying on myself, as usual.

The next morning Doug's nowhere to be seen and Tricity seems to have decided I'm not interested in him.

"You helped rescue my father," she says, half-questioningly.

That overstates my involvement, but modestly I agree. Miss Nice Guy, that's me. Always like to tell people what they want to hear. I ought to have been a politician.

She takes me on a conducted tour of the factory. By daylight the scrapyard has turned into an industrial ant-heap.

"There are more people here than I expected from what the Earthers said," I tell her.

"The Steam-master has brought the Durnovaria and Blandford Forum factories here." She waves her arm proudly. "We will surprise the Earthers. They do not think we are so many."

I get the impression that she never realized the Industrials' potential either.

We come across a blonde woman pouring molten metal into moulds. She is stripped to the waist and looks like the figurehead on a Viking ship.

"This is Scientist Metra from Durnovaria," Tricity says.

"What are you making?" I ask.

"Bolts," she says, panting. When the metal is all poured, she stops and wipes the sweat off her arms. "Look at this," she says lovingly, and shows me a metal contraption which means nothing to me.

"What is it?"

"A crossbow. Very powerful at short range. It can be fired one-handed if need be."

"The Steam-master invented it," Tricity says proudly.

Suddenly the reality of what's going to happen becomes real.

Metra caresses the weapon. "We've tested it on sheep. A bolt fired square buries itself eight centimetres deep. It goes through the fleece and smashes light bone. It will do the same to Rangers."

"I suppose it will," I say, and we move on.

"The Rangers killed her sister," Tricity says. "After they'd raped her, of course."

"Of course."

"They hunt us away from the towns in autumn, but want us back in the spring to trade for our metal goods."

I goof about the factory all morning. There's a sense of excitement fuelling the activity. I see Doug several times going from one work site to another, touching people, giving shoulders a pat, arms a squeeze, and being stroked almost like a talisman in return. The Industrials are amazed at themselves.

At midday all activity ceases and everyone rests until evening when scouts return from Sarum. A boy reports to Doug's tent and I recognize Vanguard. He's dressed as an Earther and has been in the city. He reports that everything is normal. Most of the harvest pilgrims have departed and everyone is looking forward to a good night's rest after the revelry.

At dusk we move out. I'm equipped with a leather outfit, trousers and jerkin, like everyone else. Doug's wearing his clothes from the Base. We're an army on the move. All Industrials aged twelve and over are taking part in the attack. Children and those unable to fight are going north across the plain – in case things go wrong.

We travel faster than the procession of carts which took me to Stonehenge. Those on foot lope tirelessly along beside the horses. We reach the city in the early hours of the morning while it's still dark.

The plan starts with the overpowering of the Watch on the city walls. Not difficult since there are not many of them, they're old and their hobby is seeing who can live the longest. The assault team ropes them up and lowers them down the wall. Doug's intention is to leave the ordinary citizens unharmed and only hit the Rangers and the city hierarchy.

Good thinking, I concede. I'd have done the same myself if I wasn't cursed with the Hamlet syndrome. I stomp up and down any handy battlement outlining plans of action but never putting them into effect. I may kid myself that I'm in control but, let's face it, Doug and Chris only did what I wanted as long as it suited them. Note for shopping list: remember to buy some ideals and charisma. Shopping. God, how I miss shops!

Part two of Doug's plan is headed "Slaughter the Rangers". Popular little number this. The groundlings love it.

The entrance to the Cathedral Close is guarded by the Rangers themselves. This is their enclave, so the serious stuff begins.

The boy Vanguard, still dressed Earther fashion, goes up to the vast double gates and stammers through a grille that he's come to work in the High Warden's kitchen. A Ranger comes out of the guard house, shines a lantern through the bars, then contemptuously pulls a catch to let him through the sally-port.

Vanguard does a bit of forelock tugging, steps through the door, turns towards the guard house and produces one of Doug's crossbows. It works perfectly. I can even hear the bone crack as the bolt goes through the Ranger's ribs. He falls back into the guard house where another Ranger says, "I say, old chap, what's going on?" or words to that effect. But by that time Metra and some other Industrials are through the outer door. Metra looks into the guard house and there's another crack. When she comes out her lips are drawn back in an ecstatic gleam. She gives Doug the thumbs-up and races after her squad, who are heading for their targets in the Close.

It's still too early for the ruling elite to be up and about and the Close is gloomy and silent. Leather-clad shadows lug sacks into the cellars of buildings or pile them by doors and shuttered windows like lethal Santa Clauses. The sacks are packed with incendiaries and oily rags to create smoke.

An insomniac Ranger steps out of one house and does an impression of a porcupine as he curls up with crossbow bolts for quills.

There's no signal given but at approximately the same moment over half the buildings in the Close burst into flames. That's a few centuries' architecture written off, I reflect. But Doug never has been a humanities person. Paddle-steamers were his thing.

Not many Rangers try to escape their blazing barracks. Overcome by smoke, I presume. Those who stagger blindly out are shot down. We have accurate plans of the Close and know precisely which buildings are Ranger accommodation.

Then it's all over. A few sparks from the holocaust have started two or three fires outside the Close and putting them out keeps the citizens happily occupied.

I wander about. No real role.

"That was the easy part," I say to Metra when I bump into her. She's still grinning wildly, obviously on a high.

"The Steam-master will know what to do next," she says.

"We might have wiped out the Rangers, but their families won't be very pleased."

Metra laughs. "Their families were in the buildings with them."

For a moment I am almost shocked. Then I remember that, although he wasn't really a humanities person, like all of us Doug did twentieth-century history.

# *THE NEW ORDER*

The Cathedral still stands, but it is surrounded now by a charred circle of burnt-out houses. Somehow that makes it more impressive.

Doug and his myrmidons have not stopped. The bonfires were only stage one of the plan, not the climax. I should have known better than to think that the next act would be left to chance.

The citizens of Sarum are herded on to the meadow surrounding the Cathedral and told to sit facing the west doors. There were cows there earlier but they've been driven out to graze on the riverbank. A semicircular space is kept clear in front of the Cathedral. Reminds me of the Stonehenge arrangement and I wonder what spectacular Doug's got up his sleeve.

The only body the people see is the High Warden's. He's lying outside his house with a crossbow bolt pinning his silk nightshirt to his chest. I find I am saddened by the sight: it's the finest material I've seen in this shop-forsaken hole. The citizens bravely conceal their grief and concentrate on worrying about themselves. A line of Doug's force surrounds the meadow.

I find Doug in the Cathedral having a chat with the Bishop, who looks as optimistic as any cleric would on Judgement Day. There's a bloody great carthorse in there as well. I wonder whether Doug's planning to have the Bishop roped to horses and torn limb from limb. The Bishop looks as though the same thought's occurred to him.

"You saw the High Warden on the way here?" Doug asks chattily.

They're sitting in the choir like cardinals planning a martyrdom.

The Bishop dabs his face with his cassock. "Indeed, I did."

"I understand he was in the habit of threatening you and your clergy?"

"I'm sorry to say that is the case – or *was*."

Doug smiles reassuringly. The Bishop swallows nervously.

"I have summoned the people in order to tell them that those days are past. It is a pity that the Cathedral is too unsafe to have them gather in here. We shall have to do something about that, shan't we?"

"Strengthen the fabric..." the Bishop suggests hesitantly.

"I am going to introduce myself to the people. I shall tell them that the tyrant has been deposed. I trust I can count on the Church's support. An appropriate quotation from scripture..."

I find myself, like the Bishop, wondering whether there is a threat in Doug's words, or whether it's all in my imagination.

The Bishop nods eagerly. "Some suitable words, indeed."

"I expect you'll want to robe yourself appropriately," Doug murmurs. "Your most impressive vestments for the occasion."

The Bishop scuttles away and yelps for his clergy to prepare him.

"Now circus for the masses," Doug tells me, laughing. "Vanguard, Tricity," he calls. "Get the horse ready."

His acolytes drape the animal in a huge cream bedsheet. I have the feeling that this was last used by the High Warden. It is a comfort to know that the appreciation of luxury has not entirely perished.

"You'll get a better view outside," Doug tells me.

I can take a hint. I try not to scuttle like the Bishop. Outside, the Earthers are glancing nervously at the Industrials' crossbows and looking as though they're hoping the audition is for the lynch mob not the victims.

Doug doesn't hurry. He allows the tension to rise. One or two of the spectators are sobbing. At last there's a grating of grit against stone, sound-effects for a horror movie, and the great west doors are dragged open by invisible hands. Then there's another pause. Good theatrical stuff.

A distant vibration begins, so slight at first that only a tongue against the Cathedral stones could have confirmed it. The vibration resolves itself into steady, plodding hoof beats. The Cathedral echoes but only darkness shows through the doors.

Eventually a girl appears. I don't recognize Tricity for a moment because she's been transformed from a grimy Industrial psychopath into a vestal virgin with a coronet of flowers. Spirit of Peace. Spirit of Puke. She's leading the white carthorse. I realize belatedly that this is one of the horses Doug stole from Werham. He'd had a chance to talk to scientist Darwin by then, but how far ahead was he thinking when he chose this one?

Doug comes into view, ducking his head to pass through the doorway. Somehow he looks bigger than ever. It's not just being on the horse. It's a carthorse, but it's not out of proportion – he needs one that size. The silk sheet that drapes the animal ripples like liquid and every inch of its harness gleams. Behind comes the Bishop, clad in red and gold, and his clergy. Last is Vanguard, Doug's pet bodyguard, I guess, with a crossbow cocked.

Doug leads the procession out of the shadow of the Cathedral and as they enter the sunlight he raises his arm. For a second I think he's holding a sceptre, and in a way he is. He's brandishing a huge, polished piston arm from some old machine. The sun glints on it and sends blinding flashes across his audience.

This is where he's going to cock it up, I think.

He's not your speech-making type. He'll mumble a few enigmatic phrases and lose it.

"Rejoice!" he cries, still holding up the piston arm. "The time of Judgement is ended!"

Not a bad opening, I concede.

"The land has been cleansed of pollution."

OK, so I'm wrong again. If I'd scripted this, there'd have been too many clauses, conjunctions and conditionals. Keep it simple, stupid. That's what the peasants want, and he knows 'cos he is one.

"Brother Soil was the last carrier of pollution. His death lifted Judgement from the land.

"The High Warden and the Rangers tried to prolong the time of Judgement. They have paid the price. No one else will die. Those who were led astray by the High Warden will be pardoned.

"The divisions in the land have been healed. There are no more Earthers or Industrials. From today you are all citizens of a new land. There will be equal justice for all."

I feel the threat in that and so does the audience.

"Bishop!"

The Bishop steps forward and as he does so one of the clergy holds up a cross on a pole behind Doug like a blessing. Neat move, I think. The Church can't allow people to go around crowning themselves. Pretend that you bestow authority on them and one day people might believe you.

"It is written," the Bishop begins, "'Behold, I send my messenger before thy face. The messenger of the new covenant in whom you will delight. And in these days the wolf shall dwell with the lamb and the leopard shall lie down with the kid. They shall not hurt or destroy for the whole earth shall be full of the knowledge of the Lord.'"

At which point Doug's mount steps forward and forestalls further quotes from the Bishop.

"You heard of me from ancient legend," Doug tells the crowd. "Beneath Silbury Hill I have slept, waiting for your call. I have waited during the time of Judgement. I have slept since last the land was pure."

The crowd nods at his words as if at an old-time sing-along. Do they really believe this? I ask myself. Then I spot Chris and Willow in the mass of faces. He is looking chagrined as usual; she is open-mouthed, lapping it up.

"I am the Bearer of Power," Doug declares, holding up the piston arm again. "Behold Excalibur!"

This is over the top. I cringe. But I'm wrong again. The crowd cheers. Is there nothing people won't believe? We know the answer to that, don't we? After all, we did twentieth-century history.

Doug raises his hand for silence.

"Today I declare a feast day. Tomorrow we start to build a new world!"

The Industrials have removed the High Warden's body and brought barrels of beer from his storehouses. They begin to distribute it liberally. Honeymoon period for the new government. Will it outlast the hangover?

I keep to the fringe of the crowd, who all seem to want to touch Doug or his horse, and wonder if there might be a demand for holy horse dung from the great liberator's charger. But he's already cornered the market in that, hasn't he?

Chris appears at my elbow like a prophet of doom. "He can't do this," he tells me stiffly. "There'll be trouble."

"That's the nature of existence," I say, being struck philosophical by his permanently sour attitude.

Chris is right, of course. As soon as the drink begins to take effect, there's a fight between an Earther and an Industrial.

Doug sails through the crowd to the scene of the fracas like a sewer rat through shit. I follow in his wake.

The crowd is suddenly subdued. Two Industrials are holding an Earther. They look relieved to see Doug, as if they expected the other Earthers to attack them and rescue their prisoner. Doug does not give the impression that such an idea could occur to him.

"Who was fighting with this man?" Doug demands.

Tappet steps forward. "He said the beer would turn sour if I poured it," he complains, like a sulky schoolkid.

Scientist Darwin is standing nearby.

"Take Tappet's crossbow and sword," Doug orders. Then he addresses the crowd. "I told you that the time of Judgement has ended. Now these two will show you what that means."

The crowd suddenly looks as happy as a lynch mob.

Doug says to Vanguard, "Bring the rope."

Has he foreseen this too? I wonder.

To the guards he says, "Bring them to the river."

Part of the crowd follows the stars of the show through a gate in the wall and out on to a spongy riverbank where a flat-bottomed boat is waiting. Others line the crenellated wall.

Chris follows me through the gate licking his lips. "Has he got all this planned?" he asks.

"Our Douggie is not the blundering dolt he likes to pretend."

The prisoners are put in the boat.

"Tie them together by their legs," Doug orders.

The prisoners end up one lying with his head in the bow and the other with his head in the stern, and their legs bound together like parallel logs in a raft. Quite frankly, I'm mystified.

Once they're trussed, Doug leans down and speaks quickly to them so that no one else hears. He obviously has the outcome planned and doesn't want them screwing it up.

The boat pushes off with Doug, the guards and the prisoners in it. When it reaches mid-stream two of the guards hold it in place with long poles.

Doug's voice carries easily across the water. "These two are going to show you that there are no more Earthers or Industrials. There is only one people, and if you do not work together, you will perish." He pauses. "Throw them in."

There's a momentary hesitation, then the guards obey.

The Earther and Tappet disappear into the muddy water. They rise spluttering, then start to sink again.

"Come on," I whisper. "Do as Doug told you."

They begin to paddle, keeping their bound legs stiff so that the water supports them.

"We're moving," the Earther gasps.

"Keep it up," Tappet pants.

The crowd joins in, cheering them on. Slowly the two men move towards the bank.

When Doug judges that they're tiring, he sends the guards in to help them to the bank. This is greeted by a cheer from both sections of the crowd.

Doug jumps out of the boat and splashes ashore. "Release them."

He lifts them to their feet and raises an arm in each hand.

"These men are the first citizens of our new world. They have shown us that we must work together. Now I give them new names, neither Earther nor Industrial. Victor and Albert."

The pair grin foolishly after their baptism, as though they have won a prize. I wonder what the significance of Doug's choice of names is. I no longer believe that anything he does is without meaning.

# *LADY OF THE MANOR*

We're living in the High Warden's mansion, which is the best address in the Close. This is one place that hasn't changed in fifty years. It was a museum when we took the sleep, now it's a working historical model.

There are servants to cook, clean, garden and empty the commodes. It has acres of uneven wooden floors polished with beeswax, carved staircases, a kitchen big enough to roast oxen, rooms with tapestries and vast stone fireplaces, and bedrooms with four-poster beds that undulate with feather mattresses and silk sheets.

Doug has established his headquarters here. I've awarded myself the second most comfortable suite of rooms. Fiona, of course, has been given the best.

Doug was right; she was unharmed, more or less. Well, put it this way: nothing had happened to her that she wasn't already familiar with. She was found in a cellar on a bed of straw. But she still looked as radiant and shampooed as the heroine in a fairy-tale. How does she manage it? Put me in a cellar and in half an hour my hair's like Medusa's after a night clubbing.

Whenever I see Fiona, she's wearing a contented expression, and Maisie, her personal maid, is sitting next to her stroking her hand. Doug has ordered Maisie, who has devoted little button eyes, to look after her, and this seems to be the schmuck's greatest pleasure in life. I use Maisie for menial tasks, but I come a distant second to Fiona.

They spend hours sitting on a chaise longue in the window of her upstairs sitting-room overlooking the rose garden. Fiona can talk, for want of a better word, so if Brother Soil did give her the gobstopper drops, their effect has worn off. Not that that helps much when it comes to coherent conversation.

I've tried grilling her a couple of times in an attempt to find out what happened to her and what suspicions, if any, the High Warden had about us. I want to know if Chris and I were being watched or if I was just normally paranoid. "How goes it, Fiona?" I ask her chummily each time we meet.

"My father has returned," she tells me radiantly.

"Great," I say. "Now think hard. Can you remember what the High Warden asked you?"

She treats me to a goofy smile.

I persist: "Do you remember the fat slob in the dressing-gown?"

"Robin came back. He pinched me where he shouldn't."

I remember from our girly chat at the Base that Robin was her stepfather. I surmise, psycho-analytically, that she's identifying the High Warden with Robin and that his cross-examination included a physical, just like step-papa used to give her.

"OK," I say encouragingly. "Then what happened?"

"My father sent Robin away and we're together again."

For father read Doug. I should like to think that we're into fantasy incest here on Fiona's part, but Doug does not seem to think of her in that way. I do not know how he *does* think of her. Why does he bother with the fey cow at all? Is she the mystical source of his power? A sort of Lady of the Lake? Beats me.

Whatever role she plays in Doug's psyche has to remain an enigma since the conquering hero is not giving interviews and doesn't come home at night. All I know is that he's somewhere out on the Plain of Sarum with his new model army. From the information I pick up, he's welding a force out of Earthers and Industrials.

There's been non-stop activity in the three weeks since he took over. To replace the Rangers he's had each street elect its own constable, on the lines of vote for your local sheriff. He's started construction work to provide fresh water for the city and to take sewage out. It seems that when he went to the Base before rescuing Darwin (evolution in reverse there), he made laminated copies of maps and plans showing old roads, railways, waterways – the infrastructure of an industrial society. He's going to rebuild civilization, but without consulting me.

The only worry Doug seems to have is that news of what happened at Sarum will spread to other towns before he's ready to offer them his protection. So movement out of the city is restricted at present.

Only Fiona is free to do as she likes. Some days she goes walkabout in Sarum. The people worship her. I've seen them kissing the hem of her dress. She lays on hands, cures lepers, raises the dead, walks on water and kisses babies. Nauseating.

I let Fiona and Doug pursue their personal obsessions while I luxuriate in bathfuls of hot water. The taps don't work, of course, but Maisie is there to lug heated jugs up from the kitchen while I wallow. She's pleased to serve; it's what she understands.

"More water, Maisie," I instruct from the depths, "and be sure it's hot this time."

"Yes'um," she says, and curtseys.

I take it she means "Yes, madam", which is as it should be. I'm quite fond of Maisie, as one is of a dog. It's the one thing to recommend this benighted hole: people do at least appreciate social distinctions.

When I go out I take my bodyguard with me. He's a sly ex-Earther. I know he's on the make, and he knows I know. We understand each other fine, and as long as it is to his advantage to support us I can rely on him. His name was Silt. I renamed him Sam, but it wouldn't stick, so he remains Silt, which somehow sums him up.

I don't need a bodyguard, but I feel that having one gives me status. The people I meet fawn on me and I bestow a word here, an encouraging nod there. I feel like kicking them. Some people are only comfortable as victims. I am reminded of an occasion when a teacher appealed to our better natures to prevent bullying. It was a good speech and we all felt nobly supportive of the cause until we discovered who the victim was. Then our sympathy evaporated because we all knew that kicking the whining creep was really a kindness, since being a victim was the only social role he was comfortable in. Now I've got a whole townful of victims.

I use Silt as my spy to keep an eye on Chris and Willow. They only stayed in the High Warden's mansion for two days, then moved to a house next door to a disused chapel. I wondered what they were up to and one morning, about a week after they left, Silt sidles up to tell me that Chris is preaching to the people.

I say, "Let's go get ourselves some old-time religion," and Silt shows me the way.

I expect Chris to be finished by the time we get

there, but he's still going flat out, and Willow is standing nearby looking inspired and tossing in hallelujahs whenever he needs to draw breath.

When I arrive he's telling a large crowd: "The only pollution in the land comes from those who oppose the word of the Lord. Did not God send his only son to show us how to live?"

Willow shouts, "Hallelujah!" and so does a large contingent in the crowd.

"No one can say, 'We did not know. We were not told.' Do you want me to tell you what life in Paradise Earth will be like?"

I shout, "Yes, yes! Praise the Lord!"

"But why do you need me to tell you?" Chris asks, making chopping gestures with his hand. "You know already because the Lady Fiona has shown you. Is there anyone here who has been healed by her blessed touch?"

Voices are raised praising St Fiona of the Lobotomy.

"In Paradise Earth there will be no more sin or sickness, no hunger or suffering. Neighbour will live at peace with neighbour."

More Hallelujahs.

"Let all those amongst you who would enter Paradise Earth follow me to the river to be baptized into a new life."

The crowd surges away after him. A good wash is what most of them need. Is this Chris's personal bid for power? I wonder. Hearing his sermon, I'm not surprised I never got a handle on him.

I decide to mention to Doug what Chris is up to because I don't intend to let a repressed evangelical get in the way of modern plumbing. However, I can't immediately, since Doug is still away playing soldiers.

I'm being sidelined all right. Whenever I think about this I start to worry about the rest of the sleepers in the Base. When are the next lot due to wake up? I can't remember. I've lost all track of time. But someone ought to be there to greet them, and since none of the others is interested, it has to be me.

This is all an excuse. Actually, I'm suffering from terminal boredom. There are no shops worth the name, I've got nothing to do and no one loves me. If only Ralf were here it would all be different. As it is, I'm surplus to requirements.

The morning after Chris's sermon, Silt tells me that the army is not nearby on the plain after all and apparently hasn't been for two days. Where is it? No one knows.

On a hunch I listen to the radio at the old time that evening.

The first thing that comes through is Doug's voice saying: "We've captured Durnovaria."

"You mean you've taken another town?" I ask, stunned into feeble-mindedness. "By force? Over."

"Got it in one," Doug laughs. I feel that he's called me because he wants to tell someone who will appreciate the enormity of his achievement. The people with him don't know him as anything other than Alexander the G.

"We failed to stop news of what happened in Sarum spreading, but it turned out to be our strongest weapon." He laughs again. A big kid with toy soldiers.

Events conspire to aid some people, I think bitterly.

"The news caused panic. When we rolled up with a steam catapult it only needed one round to smash the town gates and they surrendered. They were so eager to hand over the Rangers we had to stop them from lynching them."

Shocking the way these primitives behave.

"What now? Over."

"I told you this society was hollow," he rattles on. "No aim beyond opposing an extinct enemy. Government is fragmented. Each Warden is interested only in his own survival. No co-operation. One push and and the whole sham collapses. Now I'm going to rebuild."

I remember again the paddle-steamer he constructed. The Steam-master.

"But build what? Over."

More laughter. "I'm going to start the Industrial Revolution, of course. Coal, iron, steam. I shall be pushing down into the West Country and up into the Midlands to secure supplies of iron and coal. I'll soon have a single-track railway working. A lot of the old skills have been passed on. Devotion to Earther life was only skin deep."

"Chris has started to hold religious meetings," I

tell him, inconsequentially. I can't think what else to say. "Over."

"Ask him if he'd like to be Archbishop of Wessex. Wait!"

I hear voices in the background. Then Doug's laugh, like a monomaniac who can suddenly indulge his favourite perversion without check.

"A messenger has just arrived," he announces. "Blandford Forum begs me to take the town under my protection. They've executed their squad of Rangers to show their sincerity."

"What about the sleepers?" I say. "It must be nearly time for their early morning call. Over."

"I've no time for them and they're no use to me. My people have to learn for themselves. Progress is evolutionary – you can't jump steps. So it's the Age of Steam first." He pauses. "Here's what I want you to do. Release the news that Durnovaria and Blandford Forum have joined us. Then I want you to go back to the Base and alter the settings on all the resuscitation programmes. There's no point in the sleepers waking yet. Take an armed escort with you to Werham. You can accept the town's submission on the way. Out."

"Over and out," I say redundantly, which seems appropriate for me.

# *THE SLEEPERS*

I scramble out of a stream and up a bank. Clay and decaying vegetation liquify under my weight. I grab a root to stop myself sliding back. There's an unvarying drizzle. Where's the bloody Base gone?

It never occurred to me that I might not be able to find the place. How long have I been in this world? I've lost count; Doug's the only one with a watch.

I stagger on, panting, "Bugger Doug with a steam catapult" in time with my footsteps. I'm soaked through. The front of my dress is as sodden as my shoulders, the heels of my apologies for shoes slip off with every step and I'm too exhausted to push my slimy hair off my face. I'm only warm so long as I move. I daren't stop. Water is a better conductor than cloth, therefore I lose body heat faster than I produce it. Why do I hear all my defunct teachers lecturing me in McKay's voice?

I make it to higher ground and stumble in what I hope is the right direction. A salt mist is singing in from the sea. Mould-covered walls appear without warning. If I don't find the Base soon, I'll end up draped over one of them like limp washing. I clamber over obstacles, breaking my nails and grazing my ankles. I'm stung and prickled because wherever I choose to climb there's a patch of rank growth waiting for me on the other side.

Then I think I hear breathing. Something's following me. It takes big, slow, easy breaths as it flows over obstacles. You're imagining it, I tell myself.

What happened to zoos? I suddenly wonder. When the Collapse came, did some animal rights nutters release all those furry killing machines? Is one of their offspring shadowing me in the mist? I've seen wild pigs. Do they eat people? Pigs eat anything. Not people from the computer age. I find a stick and a hand-sized lump of rock and feel better. That proves how technologically advanced I am. But the breathing feels nearer.

There's nothing there, I tell myself. Yes, there is, myself answers. It's just behind you. Out of sight in the mist. It's got fetid breath. It's raw nature. It knows no rules. It rends and tears. It's a childhood nightmare come to life.

I flee in total, exhausted panic towards a shadowy mass which rises in front of me. Get up high. Climb a tree. Gibber. Nothing like instinct when shit-scared. Do I recognize that rock? Is it the Base door? I hear a strange sobbing sound. Where's that coming from? The mist thickens. I can't see a thing. The sound rises. I cling to a rock. Christ, it's me! Just out of puff, that's all. Panting. I'm not the hysterical type. Never admit to weakness, that's my cracker of a motto. What's there to be hysterical about? Ralf. Dad. Suzy. Brother Soil. Am I mourning? Nah. The sobbing subsides. The mist thins again. See, there's nothing there. It's all in the mind. Only shadows. Everything's all right: I'm alive.

I try talking to the rock. "Freedom," I tell it. That's a laugh. When I chose that word there was hope.

The door of the Base opens smoothly. I drag myself through, drop my clothes in a trail down the corridor and crawl naked into my foetal-shaped sleepsac.

The next morning things look different.

A shower. Shampoo. Depilatory cream. Deodorant. Body spray. Mouthwash. Lotions. This is what life's about. The easy cleanliness of the twenty-first century.

So what am I going to do? Not go back to the outside world, that's for sure. Doug and Chris may be happy building their empires, and Fiona's delirious in lu-lu land, but I'm not going to live without all the comforts of the Base. Not to mention medicine. We've been lucky not to get ill. How long do all the shots we were given last? I don't want to grow old in a society where there are no cures for Alzheimer's, Parkinson's or cancer, and I simply can't live without anaesthetics and synthetic organ transplants.

I have a holiday. I pamper myself. I watch videos on the giant screen in the assembly hall and play music full-blast over every speaker in the Base. I didn't realize how much I'd missed the media. Culture outside is at an end except, appropriately, for morris dancing, which has always been an activity for the brain-dead.

When I'm feeling human again I decide to get down to business. What am I going to do? First, explore the Base properly. I never really did before we left, and all I've done since I got back is make use of the programmes I've needed and looked at the sleepers when I've wanted some undemanding company.

So I go walkabout to find answers. We were too sure we knew what we were up to at the start. If we were supposed to emerge into a world reborn after the virus, why are there enough provisions to survive indefinitely? I seem to remember Chris asking that. The store tunnel contains every tool ever invented. It also contains a rack which is pulled across another tunnel entrance to conceal it.

Why? Who? Doug! The answer accompanies the question. I'd accepted his statement that the store tunnel was all. Why'd he lied? To get an edge? How long back had he been planning his coup d'état?

I shift the rack with difficulty. Great ox! I discover tunnel flowing from tunnel. All silver coated. All stuffed with more advanced equipment. They illuminate themselves as I pass, and lead ever down. I end up leaning over a railing looking into a cavern in the hollow heart of the hill. It is a dream of destruction, a military emporium, a massive arsenal of cocooned shapes.

No weapons! The bastard lied from the start. We'd been sitting on enough equipment to launch World War III. Doug knew, but it didn't suit his plans to share the knowledge.

I touch nothing and return to the accommodation level to think out my plans. The sleepers are mine. Still a few weeks till they wake. They lie as peaceful as embryos in their capsules, waiting for me to deliver them. My dragon's teeth.

I'm going to trust only myself from now on. But really, this time. No more Miss Nice Guy. First thing to do is secure the Base against Doug et al. I go to the control room and call up "Functions" and locate "Base Security". I find "Passwords" and wipe out all except my own.

There's a flicker of light from behind the screen. I realize that the computer has just checked my retinal identity.

At which point I lose control, and the screen melts into a 3-D image of a man's face which I think I ought to recognize, like someone briefly famous after a disaster. I wait and feel my palms are damp.

"Congratulations, Cindy." The face smiles confidently. "You have successfully completed the first part of your mission."

"*Pause,*" I say. The words sink in. All smiles look false when frozen.

I shrug. "*Play.*"

"I am the Vice Chancellor of the University," the face reminds me. "At this stage in your mission it is judged to be safe, psychologically, to provide you with an explanation of your situation."

I slide down in my chair and put my feet on the console.

"You and your parents were given the impression that Project Hibernation was solely to ensure your survival in the face of the diseases resulting from the Mexico Virus. This was not wholly untrue."

I can recognize mealy-mouthed university-speak when I tread in it.

"Those of us on the Hibernation Committee calculated that if certain groups gained control as a result of the chaos occasioned by the virus, the centre would not hold and society would fragment. You will know by now that that is precisely what happened.

"Thus we come to your present situation. It was estimated that by the time you woke, society would be in a state of collapse and ripe to begin the climb back to the technological civilization you knew. Your entry into what, to you, would be a barbaric society would provide the impetus necessary to begin the process."

"*Pause.*" I take a deep breath and study the fat, academically pale face. I'm just a specimen in his experiment. "You're the bastard who condemned me to the last three months' slave labour. You could have got me killed, like you did Ralf. How ruthless can you get?" I blow him a kiss. A control freak after my own aspirations. "I love you, you swine," I tell the VC. "*Play.*"

"Since you wish to erase the keywords which allow entry to the Base, it is clear that one or more members of your team is established in the society you discovered. Please would you comfirm this, Cindy?"

"Correct," I say. I like the personal touch. Makes you feel needed.

"Your fellow team members were chosen because their psychological profiles suggested that they would react in particular ways advantageous to rebuilding our society. The spontaneity of all your reactions was important, which is why there was no message to forewarn you when you were resuscitated."

"*Pause,*" I snap.

There was a message, I just didn't think to look for it. Then I realize. Dad's message was his own contribution. He didn't know what was really happening, so he stuck his sentimental oar in as usual and could have blown everything. Now whose side am I on?

"*Play.*"

"Please indicate which members of your group have successfully established themselves outside the Base."

I inform the face that Doug and Chris have made it, then add Fiona as an afterthought. The expression does not flicker.

"In the light of the information you have just supplied the resuscitation dates for all the other sleepers will be adjusted automatically. Instructions for your own re-hibernation follow this message. Good luck, Cindy."

Do I detect a dry tone to the valediction?

So all is clear, I reflect. The choice of the five of us was deliberate, not a cock-up. Ralf was supposed to get himself killed to give us a shot of adrenalin. Fiona had to crack up to precipitate us into action. Doug is the builder. Chris is the preacher of moral guidelines.

And what about little ole me? What capability led to me being chosen? What am I good at? Self-deception, that's what. I'm a failed control freak who kids herself that she's in charge of events. But I was teamed with two monomaniacs and a nut-case whom I had no hope of controlling. So since there was nothing in this poxy epoch for me to control, I was bound to run back to the security of the Base where I could rule a whole world of my own.

That was my role in the team: to fail in the outside world and run home to Daddy VC to confirm the stage the Hibernation Programme had reached.

Yep, I did deserve my place on the team after all. Nice to know what people think of you.

Now there's only one thing left to do. The VC has me figured out all right, down to the last little glitch in my personality profile. I *am* going to jump again. So this is my message in a bottle to myself. See you in the twinkling of an eye.